High Karate

Only the edge of my right eye had caught the action, but her move had been such a blur that it took me a few seconds to piece together how it had gone down. As Brady had lunged, she had twisted into the air and both her feet had lashed out at him as she came round. And then, I swear, she had done a back flip and landed on her feet with the gun pointing at me.

She had done it; she was the real thing. She had taken out Brady. You want to know something terrible? At the back of my mind there was just the faintest bit of satisfaction at his being taken down by a girl. I was chasing a teenage punk up a flight of stairs when I had my heart attack, and I knew that although everybody wished me well, they all figured that this kind of thing would only happen to a wussy. Even Brady looked kind of funny whenever he mentioned it. Now he was lying on the rug gulping in great gasps of air while the woman who downed him was standing there with not a hair out of place. I couldn't help it.

"Lady," I said, "you are something."

"Bass lets it all hang out when he writes; a nice mix of stylish suspense, sex, and slapdash action. He scares you, too. . . ."

—*Boston Globe*

Books by Milton Bass

The Half-Hearted Detective
The Broken-Hearted Detective

Published by POCKET BOOKS

For orders other than by individual consumers, Pocket Books grants a discount on the purchase of **10 or more** copies of single titles for special markets or premium use. For further details, please write to the Vice-President of Special Markets, Pocket Books, 1230 Avenue of the Americas, New York, NY 10020.

For information on how individual consumers can place orders, please write to Mail Order Department, Paramount Publishing, 200 Old Tappan Road, Old Tappan, NJ 07675.

THE Broken-Hearted Detective

A VINNIE ALTOBELLI MYSTERY

Milton Bass

POCKET BOOKS
New York London Toronto Sydney Tokyo Singapore

The sale of this book without its cover is unauthorized. If you purchased this book without a cover, you should be aware that it was reported to the publisher as "unsold and destroyed." Neither the author nor the publisher has received payment for the sale of this "stripped book."

This book is a work of fiction. Names, characters, places and incidents are products of the author's imagination or are used fictitiously. Any resemblance to actual events or locales or persons, living or dead, is entirely coincidental.

An *Original* Publication of POCKET BOOKS

POCKET BOOKS, a division of Simon & Schuster Inc.
1230 Avenue of the Americas, New York, NY 10020

Copyright © 1994 by Milton Bass

All rights reserved, including the right to reproduce
this book or portions thereof in any form whatsoever.
For information address Pocket Books, 1230 Avenue
of the Americas, New York, NY 10020

ISBN: 0-671-74243-4

First Pocket Books printing November 1994

10 9 8 7 6 5 4 3 2 1

POCKET and colophon are registered trademarks of
Simon & Schuster Inc.

Cover art by Ben Perini

Printed in the U.S.A.

*For Ruthie
and the Gang:
Michael, Elissa, Amy,
Donna, Joe, Tobey*

1

According to the pilot, the temperature was a hundred and six degrees when we landed in Tucson, and as soon as we stepped out of the terminal building, I could feel parts of my body sticking to each other in a way that almost hurt. Brady started shaking his pants like he had fleas in them.

I'd been to Arizona once before, to pick up a prisoner, but it had been only a hundred and one degrees that time. The Arizonians tell you that the temperature doesn't matter because it's dry heat, but dry or wet, anything over a hundred degrees makes you feel close to puking if you're not used to it. As a matter of fact, I don't see how anybody could ever get used to it. Maybe my Sicilian blood isn't as thin as it should be. Maybe my heart attack had made me more susceptible to temperature, but I could tell that Brady was suffering as much as I was, and his heart could run a steam plant.

"My shorts are cutting me in half," said Brady, "and soon there'll be nothing for my wife to play with when we get home."

"Let's go buy some jungle clothes," I told him.

"What for?" he asked.

"So we'll be more comfortable."

"I ain't laying out money for new clothes just because I'm going to be hot for a couple of days," he said. Brady was not what you would call a smooth dresser to begin with, and the only time he ever wore something new was after his birthday or Christmas.

"The client will pay for it," I told him.

"Look," he said, "we've got to sit down somewhere and have you tell me what the hell is going on. Who's the client, what's the job, how much money is involved, and what the hell are we doing in Tucson in the first place?"

I had meant to fill him in on the plane, but the only seats we could get at the last minute had been thirty rows apart. I wanted to get going as soon as possible, but Brady had to know the score if he was going to be more than backup muscle. When we were still on the San Bernardino police force, ninety-nine percent of our time was spent concentrating on one angle of a case and following it until we found out what we needed or that we didn't need what we found. The more Brady knew the more he could help, and I needed all the help I could get.

I told the cabbie to take us to a clothing store in town, and he let us out in front of one that looked expensive. But we didn't have any time to fool around so I led Brady through the door into a facsimile of the climate at the Arctic Circle. You could feel the sweat freeze on your body.

There were four clerks, but we were the only customers. A guy dressed like he was on his way to a fashion show drifted over to us, his eyes mea-

THE BROKEN-HEARTED DETECTIVE

suring everything, including what might be in our wallets. He would have messed his pretty pants if he'd known about the stash I was carrying in the briefcase.

"May I help you, gentlemen?" he asked, and there was in his voice what my brother Petey, the only four-year college man in the family, would have described as irony. You could tell he thought we were beyond help.

"We just flew in on business," I told him, "and we need some cool clothes more suitable for your climate. From underwear out. Two of each."

His eyes narrowed a bit as he looked us over with a different viewpoint, figuring what he could push off on grunts like us.

"There's one other thing," I said. "We need to walk out of here wearing whatever we buy."

He gave me one of those smiles.

"That would be impossible," he said. "The minimum time for tailoring is two weeks, and even that can't be guaranteed."

"Thank you very much," I said, starting to turn toward the door. "Are there any other clothing stores in this area?"

For a second he almost let us go. But the store had been empty when we came in there, and it could have been that we were the first potential customers that had walked through the door that day.

"However," he said, his face smiling but his eyes hard, "you gentlemen are obviously in an emergency situation, and our motto has always been to satisfy the needs of the customer so why don't we see what we can work out."

We worked out quite a bit with the other three

clerks assisting, plus the shop tailor who kept muttering to himself while measuring us. Finally we had a collection which came to just over fifteen hundred dollars. Because he was so big, Brady's stuff needed more altering than mine, but the clerk convinced the tailor that it could all be done in two hours.

"Okay," I told them. "We'll go out and get something to eat, and then we'll come back to pick up the clothes."

"Is this going to be cash or charge?" asked the guy who seemed to be boss, and right away I realized he was wondering if we were going to walk out the door and disappear forever.

"Cash," I told him, "and I'll give you half of it now."

"Go!" he yelled at the tailor. "These gentlemen are in a hurry."

The heat smacked into us again as we went out the door, but right across the street was a restaurant with carved wooden doors, and that made you think of coolness and comfort. When we got inside, it turned out to be exactly as the doors had promised.

"Okay," said Brady, after the waitress had taken our orders for draft beers and spaghetti with one meatball for me and four for Brady, "tell me what the hell is going down here."

2

"It's a complicated story," I said, as Brady drained his beer in one long swallow and stared toward the area where he thought the waitress might next appear, "but I'll try to keep it tight as possible, and then you can ask about whatever you want filled in."

He made a swirling motion in the air with his fingers, and then switched his eyes back to me. I figured we had another round coming.

"I can only drink this one," I said. "It doesn't mix well with my medicines."

"Don't worry about it," he instructed.

"Do you remember that nurse I had in intensive care?" I asked. "The pretty one? Betty Wade?"

"You son of a bitch," he exclaimed, loud enough that I turned my head to see who else might have overheard. "You scragged her, didn't you? Right there in the fucking room with all those tubes and crap stuck in you? Jesus! You go in there with a heart attack and you come out with a scalp tied to your belt. Here my wife is saying novenas for you, and I'm worried half out of my mind and trying to convince the captain that it should be an inspector's funeral, and you're boffing the nurse. Jesus Christ Almighty!"

There was such an air of wonder and respect about

5

him that I could feel my chest sticking out a little and my shoulders squaring on their own. Crazy, huh? Or maybe just plain old Italian.

"It wasn't like that at all," I told him. "It wasn't like that at all. We established a relationship after I got out of the hospital. She means a lot to me and she's in trouble, and we've got to find her and straighten out whatever the hell is wrong."

"How do you know she's in trouble?"

"She called to ask for help."

"She told you she was in trouble out here, and you said you'd come out and help her?"

"I didn't really get to talk to her. There was a message on my machine, but she was cut off before she could tell me where she was and what the problem is."

"Then how'd you know to come here?"

"Because that's where she was heading when she left San Bernardino. She was coming to work here at a hospital, but when I tracked down the one she was working at, they said she'd left a month ago, and they didn't know where she went. I talked one of the personnel people into giving me her address, but the operator said that the number was no longer in service."

"Then how do you know she hasn't left the area?"

"I don't. But this is where the trail begins, so that's where we have to start."

"What about the client and the money?"

"I'm the client," I said, "and here's the money." I patted the briefcase that was beside me in the booth.

Brady finished his second beer and pulled my unused one over for his third. He took a long look at me, thought for a moment, and then asked, "How much money is in that case?"

It was my turn to figure for a moment, not that I

THE BROKEN-HEARTED DETECTIVE

didn't want to tell him, but math was never one of my strong points. My brother Petey is the accountant in our family, and he takes care of my taxes and has many times demonstrated to me my stupidity when it comes to balancing a checkbook.

"Subtracting the money for the plane tickets and the clothes," I concluded, "something like ninety-seven thousand dollars."

Without asking my permission or pardon, Brady pulled the case to him, snapped open the locks and lifted the cover about an inch. The waitress approached with our spaghetti, and he gently closed the lid again and thumbed the locks into place. We ate our food for a while without saying a word.

"Where'd that money come from?" he finally asked.

"I earned it doing a job for a guy."

"What guy?"

"Pardo."

He drank half his beer, carefully checked how much was left, and then put his eyes back on mine.

"Tony Pardo?" he asked.

I nodded and sliced my meatball into tiny pieces to mix it in with the pasta, which was very tasty for a place like Tucson, Arizona. He looked at the case again and then back at me.

"The same Tony Pardo that burned to dust in a car crash two months ago and nobody knows from nothing?"

I dipped my head affirmatively, shaking some fake Parmesan from the glass container onto my spaghetti. I considered the hot pepper flakes in the other jar for a moment but decided against it. I liked spicy but the temperature outside had enough heat to go around.

"The same Tony Pardo who ran all the rackets?"

I nodded again, twirling my fork around the slippery strands.

"Could it be that you might have gotten that . . ." he paused to add in his own head, "hundred grand for having something to do with Tony Pardo retiring before he was ready?"

"It's a long story," I told him, "but I'll make it short. He came to me because he thought somebody in his own family was trying to kill him, and he needed a trained investigator to nose around. I went out to his house for a few days, made my report, got paid and left."

"You left before or after he started missing his Rotary meetings?"

How could I explain all that had happened to anyone who hadn't been with me to see it for himself? Brady had been my partner for nine years and was my best friend outside of my family, but I wasn't sure how I felt about myself for some of the things that had happened. I really didn't want to concentrate on it too closely.

"I left before he disappeared," I lied to Brady, adding one more thing to the list.

He chewed over what I had said and took a hopeful swallow out of his empty glass.

"I've known you a long time," he said, "and I'd trust you with my life without thinking about it. I can tell that there's more to this than you're saying, but in my gut I know you're the guy I always thought you were. If you don't feel good about what you've told me, if you know there's going to come a time when I'm not going to think you're the guy I always thought you were, then give me my ticket and I'll take the next plane back."

THE BROKEN-HEARTED DETECTIVE

Was I a crook? Was I an honest man? What about the money? Was I going to report it to the Internal Revenue, tell where I got it, and explain how it all happened? I could just see the looks on their faces. Or was it going to be my secret, and I would dole out the money carefully to live comfortably for the rest of my life? Except that I would spend every penny of it, use it all up gladly, if I could find Betty Wade safe and sound. The only important thing was to find Betty. And I needed Brady to do that.

"I'm the same guy I've always been," I told him. "I haven't changed. This money doesn't mean shit to me if we can't find Betty. What I did for Pardo was on the up-and-up even though he wasn't. I wouldn't do it again, but right now I'm glad I did it because it gives us the money to find Betty."

Brady stared right into my eyes. He had been a cop too long not to know that I was holding back, shaping the story to fit my needs rather than the whole truth. But I could read his eyes as well as he could measure mine, and I knew I could count on him to give me all and any help I might need.

"What do we do first?" he asked.

"We check into a hotel, rent a car, backtrack as far as we can go," I told him, "and investigate what comes up."

"I've never seen you this way about a girl before," said Brady. "With that Carlotta I wasn't sure for a while, but then I realized she was going to be sent down. Is this one different?"

I wasn't even going to think about what he had asked, but then it hit me. This was different. This was different from anything that had ever happened to me before. There were no *if*s or *but*s, no *maybe*s, no *we'll*

THE
Broken-Hearted Detective

sees, no beating around the bush. I wanted to spend the rest of my life with this woman. I wanted her safe and alive and happy and with her arms around my neck.

"This is the most different thing that ever happened to me in my life," I confessed, telling the whole truth this time around.

"Then," he said, shoving his huge bulk out of the booth, "let's get our new duds and go find her."

3

We finally decided it would be best to blend in with the scenery so we rented a Cadillac convertible. A guy told me a joke once about this asshole who would bring a pit bull into a bar every day and scare the hell out of everybody, including the bartender, when he tried to tell him that he couldn't bring his dog in there. One afternoon another man walks in with the weirdest looking mongrel anybody ever saw, and takes a stool near the guy with the pit bull. The pit bull immediately goes nuts and lunges for the animal next to him, who opens his mouth wide and bites the pit bull right in half. Everybody is standing there stunned until finally someone gets up the courage to say, "Hey, mister, what kind of dog is that?"

"Well," says the guy after taking a swallow of his

THE BROKEN-HEARTED DETECTIVE

beer, "before I cut off his tail and painted him yellow he was called an alligator."

That was the one problem with Brady as a detective. He was so damned big and powerful looking that he would stand out in a crowd of sumo wrestlers. I could cut off his dick and paint him yellow, but he would still be somebody that people would stare at and be afraid of. The great thing about Brady was that he was just as tough and strong as he looked, but he wasn't mean or cruel. He did lose it once in a while, and then he scared even me, but mostly he was a trained professional who did what had to be done and no more.

I figured if we stuck him in a red Cadillac convertible, it would soften his image a little, maybe fool people into thinking he was some sort of retired football player or wrestler who had invested his money wisely. He balked a little when I suggested the Cadillac, but I told him he could drive, and on one piece of road he booted it up to ninety-eight before I reminded him that we not only were no longer cops, but were also in alien territory.

"Once a cop, always a cop, Vinnie," he said. "And wherever you go, you're home. Where do we go first?"

The hospital where Betty had worked was the first stop, but the minute we mentioned her name the face we were inquiring from froze and said no information was available. We kept asking for the next level up and finally reached the point where we were told that was as far as we could go. Without any cue from me, Brady reached across the desk, grabbed the woman by the front of her blouse and pulled her halfway up from her chair. She was either too surprised or too frightened to yell.

"Look," he said. "We have the impression that you people are not taking us seriously. We're trying to find out the whereabouts of a nurse named Betty Wade who worked here. Until we do, we're not leaving."

When he opened his hand, her body didn't move an inch, stayed there half bent over. She finally pushed herself up straight.

"Wait right here," she said, and ran out of the office.

In two minutes she was back with two guys from security, both somewhere in their fifties, neither of whom looked like former cops. The lady stayed outside the door.

"You gentlemen will have to leave the hospital," the smaller of the two said. "If you don't, we will be forced to remove you."

Brady walked over and stood in front of him, and the guy had to lift his head way up in order to see Brady's chin.

"Look, friend," said Brady, "we're here on legitimate business looking for a missing person, and we're getting the runaround. Now we'd like nothing better than to get cops in on this, *real cops*. You two know damn well you're not going to budge us, and you might get hurt if you went through the motions. So I suggest you go call the real cops and get them involved in the matter. Then maybe we'll find out what this hospital is trying to cover up, and what it might mean for you two to be mixed up in it. Now get the hell out of here because we're getting impatient."

They got and five minutes later a real suit walked

THE BROKEN-HEARTED DETECTIVE

into the room, top-level management in every way. He had a smile on his face.

"Gentlemen," he said, "my name is Halloran Davis and I am vice president of community relations. There seems to be some misunderstanding going on that I'm sure we can clarify in a short period. Would you be good enough to accompany me to my office?"

As we headed for the elevator, I could see staff people looking at us with more than the usual interest in a couple of strangers walking with a company bigwig. It was as if they knew what was going down, and they were as concerned in finding out the answers as we were.

"Well, gentlemen," said Davis, sinking into his big leather chair and motioning for us to sit in the hard ones across from the desk, "they tell me you've been inquiring about a nurse named Betty Wade, who was with us for a short time and then decided to go elsewhere."

Just as we did when some smooth lawyer for a drug dealer started off by trying to establish a buddy atmosphere, neither of us answered him. He waited a long few seconds, looking from one of us to the other, but then realized it wasn't going to work.

"This is against all procedure," he said, "but I am going to show you her employment record so that you will see for yourselves that she came here on a one-year contract, but then terminated it and left of her own free will. We know nothing of her since her last day at the hospital."

He opened a folder on his desk, removed two papers from it and handed them over. Brady made no motion so I picked them up. They were the usual business office forms showing salary and benefits and such-like, including the fact that she was twenty-eight years old, which was two years more than I had estimated, and on the bottom of the second sheet was typed, "Breached contract on March twenty-third, 1994. No legal action. Employment terminated."

I reached over the desk and pulled the whole folder to me. Davis stretched out his hand to stop me, but Brady's was there to block it, and he dropped it on the desk, his fingers curled into a fist.

There were three more pieces of paper in the folder, all of them in memo form. All were signed by or addressed to a woman named Theresa Pell, Vice President of Nursing. The first one said that Wade had requested to be relieved of her private assignment, and returned to either the pediatric department, which her contract called for, or even back to intensive care as an alternative. The second one said that Pell had refused the request as directed. The third one was from accounting to Pell, and asked why nurse Betty Wade had not cashed her last two paychecks, which seemed to be screwing up the books. You could tell that the last one was written by one of those prissy little pricks who delighted in sticking a finger up the nose of another department.

"I presume you know what's in these memos?" I said to Davis, and he nodded without saying anything. "What's going on?" I continued. "A hospital like this can't be part of some conspiracy against a woman. You're not a bunch of crooks or drug dealers. What the hell is going down? You people are hiding something, and we're not leaving until we find out what it is."

"What makes you think we're hiding something?" he asked.

THE BROKEN-HEARTED DETECTIVE

"Because if you weren't, if you were on the up-and-up, there would have been cops here a half hour ago," I told him. "You don't let two guys come into your hospital and shove people around like we have."

"Maybe I should shove him personally," said Brady, standing up and looming over us like a giant redwood. "Maybe I should squeeze this guy's nuts and see what pops out."

"Look," said Davis, raising his hand as if to ward off an evil spirit, "I've told you everything I can about Miss Wade. There may be more to it than I have indicated, but I am not the one who can give you answers."

"Who is the one?" asked Brady.

"Dr. McCann, the head of medical services," he answered.

"Then let's go see him," said Brady.

"He's at a meeting in Cleveland," said Davis, "and won't be back until tonight."

"Why don't we call him?" I suggested. "We can't afford to lose time."

"He gave a lecture this morning, and attended a lunch somewhere, and then will be in transit. There is no way I can track him down in Cleveland."

"Will he come to the hospital when he returns?" I asked.

"I have no way of knowing."

"What's his flight number and time of arrival?" asked Brady.

"His secretary would have handled that, and she's away for a few days," said Davis.

"You've got all the answers, don't you?" said Brady. "I think you know where this guy is this minute. I think you could reach him right this minute. I think if we left this office, you'd be on the horn to him in two seconds. I think I'm going to hurt you real bad, and then somebody will call the cops, and then things will come out in the open. But it will be too late to do you any good."

Brady looked like he was announcing Judgment Day and Davis was a known sinner. The guy was finally scared, really scared. Tiny beads of sweat were fighting the air-conditioning and winning, and his hands trembled a little on the desk. With the mask down, you could see his mind working as he tried to determine which was worse, Brady or whatever the hell gag had been put on him by his boss.

"Listen," he finally managed, "I was really on the fringes of this whole thing. Nurse Wade did leave under extraordinary circumstances, but I was not in the loop on any of it. Dr. McCann is the only one who can answer your questions. He's the only one who knows what happened. The rest of us, and I mean all of us, just followed orders. Now you can beat me up if you want to, but I must warn you that I have a heart condition, and this whole situation is definitely not one in which a person like me should be involved."

Heart condition! The magic words. What would he say if I told him that I also had a heart condition? I had been so busy worrying about Betty that I had forgotten three of my pill times since we had left for Arizona. Should I feel sorry for this poor son of a bitch because we were both in the Cardiac Brotherhood Movement? Fuck his heart. And mine too. Our only objective was to make sure that Betty's heart was beating, and to hell with anything else.

"Look," I told him, "our worry has to do with

THE BROKEN-HEARTED DETECTIVE

Betty, not you. If something happens to you while we're trying to find out what happened to her, we won't even blink. Are you beginning to get it through your head that you're not dealing with the chamber of commerce here. We're serious and ..."

He reached into his pocket and pulled out a bottle of nitroglycerin tablets, unscrewed the cap and popped the tiny pill under his tongue. I knew what it was because I had a little bottle just like that in my right-hand pocket. The guy looked gray.

"Do you want a doctor?" I asked him.

He started to shake his head no, but then thought better of it and nodded twice. If a doctor came in, he was off the hook with us. We weren't going to do anything while a doctor was treating him for whatever the hell was happening, angina or maybe even worse. He could have been faking, but what if he wasn't? I looked at Brady and he looked back at me. Then he turned and opened the door, and the two of us went out.

"Your boss is having a heart problem," I told the secretary. "You better get a doctor for him."

As we stepped out of the elevator into the lobby, we could hear the loudspeaker system calling for Dr. Mayday on the seventh floor, which was where we had just been. I hoped the guy wasn't going to die, but I was still so pissed off at him and whoever else had taken part in whatever happened to Betty that I didn't care that much. I was already thinking ahead to whether we should stake out the hospital and wait for McCann, or go to the town where Betty had lived and see what we could find out there.

At that moment a tiny little woman, so small that she looked like she was playing nursie in her white

Milton Bass

uniform, walked by me and Brady and as she passed, she said, "Meet me on the sidewalk of the emergency driveway in twenty-five minutes." Then she was gone around a corner.

Brady and I didn't glance at her or each other until she was gone from sight. How many times had this routine been worked for us by our snitches?

"Twenty-five minutes," Brady said. "Let's get a cold soda from one of the machines there."

4

She was sporting one of those purple capes with the red lining that all nurses used to wear years ago, and looked so cute that you wanted to pick her up and give her careful hugs so you wouldn't break her. She wasn't a dwarf or anything like that; her features were as delicate as my aunt Felicia's marinara sauce. I could tell that Brady was embarrassed because her eyes were at fly level when she stopped directly in front of him. There was no beating around the bush.

"Why are you looking for Betty Wade?" she asked.

Good question. Was it because she had given me my nerve back? Because she had called for help, and I owed her? No, it was time I said out loud what I had been hiding in my brain.

"Because I love her," I answered.

Out of the corner of my eye I could see Brady's head swivel in my direction.

She nodded. Good answer.

"We can't talk here," she said. "Do you have a car?"

"In the hospital garage," Brady told her.

"Go get it," she ordered him, "and pick us up here."

He moved like you did when the captain was pissed off about something.

"Fill me in with the essentials," she said, as we watched Brady loping down the sidewalk to the garage. "From the beginning."

I sorted it out quickly.

"My name is Vincent Altobelli," I began, "and Betty was my nurse when I had a heart attack. Afterward, we got to know each other better, but she moved out here before any commitments were made. I realized when she was gone how much she meant to me, but I decided to give her time to settle down before I contacted her. Then one day on my phone tape I had a message from her saying that she needed help. But the tape ran out before she finished so I didn't know what the problem was or even exactly where she was. I called all the Tucson hospitals and finally found out she had been working at this one, but they wouldn't tell me anything. Then I located her home phone number, but the operator said it had been disconnected. So my friend and I came out here to look for her, but we got the runaround again at the hospital."

She nodded but didn't say anything.

"Is she all right?" I asked.

"I don't know," the little woman said, "but I'm ... we're damned well going to find out."

Neither of us said anything more until Brady drove up. I knew she was going to fill us in on everything she knew, and it might screw things up if we pushed her. It had taken me years, but I had finally learned that pressure is not always the way to go when you're trying to get information from somebody.

She hopped in the front seat with Brady, and it took all my willpower not to give her little ass a boost as she struggled to climb inside. Then she fed him lefts and rights until we were in some suburb of Tucson, and we pulled into the driveway of a small white house.

She unlocked the door and somehow it was surprising to find that all the furniture was regular-size. You can't judge people by their looks. Should there have been doll's furniture in there?

"You men hungry?" she asked, after throwing her cape on the couch.

"I'm always hungry," said Brady.

Without saying another word she led us into the kitchen, which was also of regular dimension, but which had all kinds and sizes of step stools scattered around.

"Spaghetti all right?" she asked.

"Eat it all the time," said Brady.

A big pot of water was put on to boil, two jars of canned spaghetti sauce fished out of the cupboard and dumped into a pan, and then she cradled three cans of beer off a shelf in the refrigerator. We all sat down at the kitchen table, her on the top rung of a step stool, waiting for the water to bubble. She sucked down half that can of beer before she turned to us.

THE BROKEN-HEARTED DETECTIVE

"I get thirsty on the job," she said. "I drink and pee all night when I get home."

You could tell from Brady's face that he liked this woman. I hoped he wasn't going to toss her up in the air.

"What do you know?" she asked.

"She was coming out here to work as a pediatric nurse," I said, "because she felt she had been burned out in ICU. She told me she would get in touch after she settled in, but the call for help was the first I heard from her. I figured this was the only place we had to start from."

She nodded, finished off her beer, amazed both of us by crumpling the can in half in her little hand, hopped off the stool, got another beer and climbed up again. I could tell that Brady was thinking about divorcing his wife and moving to Tucson.

"My name's Bridget Burns," said the woman, and sat back waiting.

"As I said, I'm Vinnie and that's Matt Brady," I told her.

"She mentioned you," said Bridget, and I could feel my heartbeat rev up. She had mentioned me. I reached in my pocket, pulled out my pill case and washed the tablet down with beer.

"You're on Cardene," said Bridget.

"That's how I got to meet Betty," I told her.

"When she reported for work, they told her they had a shortage of ICU nurses," said Bridget, "which was true, and she would have to work there until they could dig up some replacements. That's how I got to meet her, and we liked each other right off. She didn't want to work in ICU, but she was a nurse, and if

21

that's where she was needed, that's where she would work. And she was doing all right until he came in."

She waited for me to say, "Who's he?"

"That's the interesting part. We never found out. This guy came in with a knife wound in the chest, and there were all kinds of bodyguards cluttering up the place, and Dr. McCann took over the case personally until some other doctor flew in from somewhere, and nowhere on the guy's chart did it list his name. They didn't even bother with John Doe. It was left blank. We all figured he had something to do with the government, but nobody in his whole gang ever said anything to anybody. They were all wearing guns under their jackets, and there would be two of them in the room with him, another four or five in the family room, and one of the orderlies told me that a lot more were scattered all over the place."

"Did you recognize his face from the newspaper or television?" asked Brady.

"He didn't look like anybody we'd ever seen in the news."

"Describe him," I told her.

"Good-looking man somewhere in his late forties. Eyes, blue eyes, that could burn a hole in your head. About five feet, ten inches. Maybe a hundred and fifty-five pounds. Blood pressure normal even though he might have been dead instead of lucky, and all the tests showed he was in good shape. Calm as hell. Knife wound missed his heart by maybe an inch, but you knew he wasn't thinking about it anymore. Betty and I were on duty when they sent him up from emergency, and sick as he was, he looked at her like he was going to take her right into bed with him. She

THE BROKEN-HEARTED DETECTIVE

knew something was peculiar about him, and it scared her."

I could feel my fingers curling into fists.

"Then what happened?" I asked.

"Just let me dump the noodles in," she said, and I sat there while she did her work and Brady pulled another beer from the refrigerator.

"He came along nicely," she said, after climbing back up on the stool, "and they moved him down to the one private suite in the hospital. Betty was assigned to be his day nurse."

"They took her out of ICU and put her down with him," I echoed. "How did she feel about it?"

"She told them she didn't want to do it," said Bridget, "but Dr. McCann himself put pressure on her. 'Just get him well enough to leave,' he told her, 'and I'll transfer you to pediatrics right away.' She couldn't afford to quit, what with her rent and car payments, so she took it on, but each day was worse than the one before."

"In what way?" I asked.

"He started telling her that he wanted her to come and live with him," she said. "A lot of patients say things like that, but with him it was different. It was like he felt he owned her. And he would grab on to her hand, and sometimes wouldn't let her go for ten or fifteen minutes. She got more scared every day."

"How long did this go on?" asked Brady.

"Almost two weeks. Then he moved back to the Venture Canyon resort where it turned out he had been staying when he was stabbed. One of the ambulance drivers told us that. When he was due to leave, he told Betty he wanted her to come with him and supervise his recuperation, that she would have her own suite at the hotel, but she wouldn't do it even for all that money."

"All what money?"

"He said he'd give her five thousand dollars a week."

"Jeez," said Brady, looking at me, "you and your girlfriend have got quite a pay scale for yourselves."

He was still unhappy about me and Pardo, but I didn't have time to worry about that.

"What did she tell him?"

"She told him there wasn't enough money in the world to get her to go with him."

"How do you know all this?"

"I was her only real friend since she got here. The first day we worked together we hit it off, and she didn't have time to make any more before she disappeared. There was just me and Adele."

"Who's Adele?"

"Adele Wilkins, her landlady."

"Would she know where she is?"

"No. We talk every day. She's just as worried as I am. A person like Betty wouldn't just leave all her things in the apartment and go off. Adele can't afford to have the place empty, but she doesn't know what to do with Betty's stuff."

"She didn't take anything with her?"

"She went in her car, but all her clothes and the furniture she bought are still there."

"Has anybody gone to the police?"

"Adele called and they told her she had to come down to the station and fill out a missing person form. So she did it, and they said they'd get back to her, but they never did. So we both went to the police station, and the chief himself came out to tell us that they had looked into it, and there was nothing suspi-

THE BROKEN-HEARTED DETECTIVE

cious, and we should let him know when she turned up again. We told him something was terribly wrong, but he said this happens all the time, people go off for one reason or another, but then they eventually show up again. He asked us if we had contacted any of her family, but we don't know about her family. I started yelling at him, but he just walked away, and they wouldn't let us in to see him. I went to the police here, but they said it was out of their jurisdiction. I asked the sergeant to at least call the chief in Rancon, and he finally did, but he got a funny look on his face while he was listening to whoever he was talking to. When he hung up, he told me that the Rancon police were handling the case, and there was nothing he could do. I asked him if something was wrong, and he thought about it for a few seconds, and then he said that was all he could tell me. That I would have to check with the Rancon police if I wanted to know any more."

"When was the last time anybody saw her?" Brady asked.

"April third," said Bridget. "It was a Monday. The flowers had just come and—"

"What flowers?" I asked.

"The flowers from him. He sent her bouquets every day, and expensive presents except she didn't open them after the first couple of times. They were all piled in her living room."

"Are they still there?"

"All of them. Except for the flowers. Adele threw the flowers away."

"What did Betty do that day after the flowers came?"

"She said she'd had enough, and she was going out

to Venture Canyon and tell him to leave her alone once and for all."

"Did you tell the police about her going out there?"

"Yes, we did."

"Did you ask them about it afterward?"

"Yes. They said they'd checked out there, and nobody had seen her."

"Did you tell them about the guy, and how she was afraid of him?"

"Yes, we did all that. But the chief said that nothing checked out, and she wasn't there."

"Is the man still there?"

"We don't know. We don't know his name so wouldn't know who to ask for."

"Do you think she might be there?"

"We don't know that either. Adele and I talked about going to the canyon, but we haven't done it. I don't see how they could keep her a prisoner. It's a public place, and they have hundreds of guests and more than a thousand employees, and it just doesn't seem possible that they could have Betty locked in a closet or something without somebody finding out and doing something about it."

The sharp smell of tomato sauce burning brought us all to our feet, and nobody said anything while Bridget saved the pot, strained the pasta, dished out the plates and brought three more beers to the table. The grated cheese was one of those shakers of fake Parmesan, and the sauce tasted like canned tomato soup, but we ate it all, and she and Brady had their third beers while I was toying with my second one. I was glad none of my relatives was there to see me eat the stuff that Americans call spaghetti. Brady had three helpings.

THE BROKEN-HEARTED DETECTIVE

"Could you call this landlady and tell her we're coming out to see her?" I asked.

"No," she told me.

I just looked at her.

"She baby-sits for people, and yesterday she told me it was an overnight job, and I don't know who the people are. But she'll be home in the morning."

"Then I guess we better go find a hotel," I told Brady.

As he started to unwind from the chair, she said, "Why don't you just bunk down here?" We looked at her.

"I've got a spare room with two beds in it," she said, "and you won't be a bother, and I'd like the company, and you'd save your money."

So the three of us watched a couple of hours of television with me hardly noticing what the hell was on, and then she led us upstairs to her guest room where there were twin beds. She gave us towels and said she wasn't due at work until noon so there was no hurry about getting up. The landlady should be back at her house by ten, and she'd call her then.

"We have to go see that Dr. McCann first thing in the morning," I told her, "so we'll let ourselves out."

"I'll call Adele and tell her you're coming then. Let me know what you find out."

When he came back from the bathroom, Brady started stripping off his clothes and looking at me. I wasn't paying that much attention, my mind working on other things.

"So it finally happened," he said.

"What?"

"You. You're in love."

"So?"

"I never thought I'd live to see the day."

"What's such a big deal?"

"You're so busy combing your hair all the time that I never thought you'd share a mirror with anybody."

"You're very funny."

"Hey, Vinnie. We'll find her. We'll find her and bring her back with us, and you'll get married and have more babies than even your brother Dominic."

"Go to sleep."

As I lay there in the dark listening to him try to shrink his body enough to be comfortable in a bed that small, I took no pleasure in his discomfort. All I wanted was to find Betty and bring her home and marry her and have more kids than even my brother Dominic.

5

The information lady told us Dr. McCann's office was on the fifth floor. The receptionist behind the desk asked our names, and then told us to go right in without even checking to see if it was all right. Brady and I looked at each other before moving. Our vibes were such that if it had been a possibly lethal operation, we would have pulled our guns, kicked in the door and rolled inside with our fingers right on the triggers. But all that was supposed to be waiting for us was Dr.

THE BROKEN-HEARTED DETECTIVE

McCann, the head of the hospital medical services. It seemed he was expecting us.

He wasn't the only one. Standing on opposite sides of his desk were two policemen, one a sergeant and the other a lieutenant. They didn't say anything, but there weren't any "Welcome to Tucson" smiles on their faces either.

Dr. McCann, on the other hand, looked almost jovial. A big, ruddy-faced man with a shock of white hair, you could understand how patients would put their trust in him. He stood up to greet us.

"Mr. Altobelli," he said, nodding at me. "Mr. Brady," he went on. "This is Lieutenant Peterson of the Tucson Police Department, and this is Sergeant Renzi. It is my understanding that you created somewhat of a ruckus during your stop here yesterday so the chief sent these two officers to monitor your visit today."

I nodded at each of the cops in turn, but only the sergeant nodded back. The lieutenant figured he was going to have to act the prick so he was getting an early start.

"I understand," said McCann, "that you two gentlemen are trying to locate a nurse named Betty Wade who worked here for a short time and is reported to be missing. I'm afraid that Mr. Davis gave you all the information we have, and there is nothing more we can tell you."

"You can tell me the name of the man who harassed her while he was a patient here," I said, "and where we might locate him. We have been told of his actions, and consider him a suspect in her disappearance. She was last seen going out to the Canyon resort to tell him to stop bothering her, and she hasn't been seen since."

"We've looked into all that," said the lieutenant, "and as far as we've been able to make out, nobody saw her there. She never got there."

"What's the name of the man she went out to see?" asked Brady, and I could tell that he was upset because he knew the cops were there to hinder rather than help us.

"We can't give you that information," said the lieutenant.

"What the hell is going on here?" I said, feeling the blood rise in my face. Easy, I told myself. Cool. Play it cool.

"Nothing's going on," said the lieutenant. "Her disappearance was reported. Chief Hellawell of Rancon looked into it, and we've looked into it, and we've found nothing. She must have left the area, and I would advise you two to do the same. There is nothing you can do here."

"Jesus Christ," exploded Brady. "We're cops, man, just like you. My friend's girl is missing and instead of trying to help us, you're giving us the kind of bullshit handed out by politicians. Can't you get it through your head? This man's a cop and his woman is missing. We're detectives and we smelled the stink of this all the way to California. Do you think you're going to tell us to leave and we'll roll over and play dead? Maybe that's how you do it in Tucson, but you ought to be ashamed of yourselves."

The lieutenant's face was getting as red as mine must have been, but I broke in before anybody could get pushed.

"Dr. McCann," I said, "we know about the guy with

THE BROKEN-HEARTED DETECTIVE

the knife wound, we know about you making Betty take care of him and the promise you made her when you ordered her to do it. We know about him harassing her and trying to scare or bribe her into coming with him, we know about the things he did after he left the hospital. You're a doctor, man, a doctor. It's your job to heal people, not make them disappear. Just give us the name of the guy, and we'll take it from there."

"I'd like to help you," said McCann and there was something in his face that made me feel he meant it, "but my hands are tied."

"If nothing else works," I told them, "we'll go to the newspapers and the television and radio stations and tell them what we know, and how you people are trying to cover it up."

"You can't do that," said the lieutenant. "It could be dangerous."

Brady walked over and planted himself in front of the man.

"You gonna arrest us?" he asked. "You gonna make us disappear? Why don't you and me figure out right now who's gonna do what to who?"

The lieutenant was a big man, but he didn't twitch an eye, knowing that Brady could break him in half before the twitch was finished. But he wasn't afraid either.

"Gentlemen," said McCann. "Gentlemen. We are just as concerned about the welfare of the young lady as you are. But there are other factors involved, and other people must be consulted before any further steps can be taken. Tell me where you are staying, and I will get back to you by this evening, hopefully with more information."

"Name me a hotel," I told him.

"What?"

"Give me the name of a hotel and we'll get a room there."

"Ah. The Pelican. The Pelican is very nice. And the prices are quite modest in the off season."

"Okay. We'll be waiting there," I told him.

"Sergeant," said the lieutenant, "escort these people to their vehicle."

We didn't bother saying good-bye, and the sergeant followed us out the door. He didn't say anything all the way to the car, but just as we were about to get in, he spoke.

"Listen," he said, looking everywhere but at us, "this is bigger than just local. Word came down that we were to stay out of it."

"From the state?" asked Brady.

"Bigger," he answered. "I don't know exactly what outfit, but it's federal. Big-time federal."

"Thanks, brother," said Brady, as he climbed behind the wheel.

"Is there anything else?" I asked.

"That's all I know. Good luck."

He turned and walked away.

"See," said Brady, as he pulled out of the lot, "cops are the same everywhere." He thought about it for a second. "Except for that prick of a lieutenant," he said. "He's the one proves the rule."

6

The first thing I did after we walked into the hotel room was call Bridget Burns. The answering machine said she was not there, but if it was Vin calling, the number for Adele Wilkins was 555-6729, and please call back if anything new was learned.

Mrs. Wilkins had been briefed on us by Bridget, but she couldn't add anything to what we already knew. I said we would keep her informed as best we could. The lady sounded so concerned about what might have happened to Betty that I started to get a strange feeling in my belly. Brady and I had worked our share of missing-person cases, and on each one you'd get a hunch about what had happened. Deep down you'd know which ones had run away never to come back, which ones were coming back and which were dead. You'd be wrong once in a while, but too often you were right, and I was beginning to have bad vibes about Betty. I rubbed my hand over my stomach, but it didn't warm up anything.

Brady came back from the toilet and threw the sports section on the bed.

"I've been thinking," he said, "and it seems to me we ought to go out to that vacation place and shake things up a little."

"The doctor promised to get back to us," I told him, "and I don't want to screw things up. If we push too hard before we know what we're doing, we might make things worse."

"We just going to sit here all day?" he asked. "Watching TV and drinking beer, and you getting nervouser and nervouser which the doctor told you ain't good for you?"

Before I could deny anything, there was a knock on the door. Brady was up like a cat with his gun out and moving to be behind the door if somebody came crashing through. I'd never seen him this jumpy. Was he feeling something that wasn't coming through to me? I walked over to the other side of the door in case somebody might pump a bullet through as an answer to my voice and said, "Yes?"

"Mr. Vincent Altobelli?"

"Yes."

"We would like to talk to you."

We. Who was we?

"About what?"

"Open the door and I'll tell you."

I had neglected to hook the chain when we had come into the room, so I did it then, stepped to the side and opened the door as far as the chain would allow. Two men were standing there, wearing suits and ties even though it had to be a hundred degrees outside.

"Yes?" I said again, my right hand curling to the side so I could get to the gun in my back holster if needed. I was coming out of my daze and starting to feel as jumpy as Brady.

"We're federal agents," said the one standing right

THE BROKEN-HEARTED DETECTIVE

in front of the door, "and we have some business to discuss with you about your visit to Tucson."

"Identification?"

He fished a badge case from his inside pocket and handed it through the door. His identification card said he was Agent Robert Yert of the Federal Bureau of Investigation, and it seemed genuine.

"What about your boyfriend?" I asked, not knowing why I was antagonizing this man even before I found out what he wanted.

They both frowned, but the second one fished out the same kind of case and handed it through. The card said he was Northrup Frye of the Central Intelligence Agency, and the face looked right but the head was bald, and this guy had quite a bit of hair on him. I looked closer and saw it was a fairly good toupee although slightly overdone. When the cards were handed back to them, they slipped them into their pockets and leaned forward in anticipation of me opening the door.

"What do you want?" I asked again.

Their faces creased again because they were not used to this kind of questioning after they had flashed their cards and badges.

"We want to come in and talk to you."

"Do you have a warrant?"

The FBI agent lost his cool, and his voice rose enough so that the other one looked around guardedly to see if anybody was within earshot.

"You're here to find out about Betty Wade," he said, "and we can tell you something about her."

I unhooked the chain and let them in. Their eyes widened a bit when they saw Brady holding his gun, but they weren't nervous. You got the feeling that they already knew a lot about us, and they weren't worried about being shot down. They surveyed the room, using their eyes and ears and noses, as all pros do, and then both of them faced me as if they knew that I was the prime factor in the hunt for Betty Wade.

"Miss Wade is alive and well," said Yert, "and the best thing you can do is go back to California and wait to hear from her."

"What do you guys have to do with this?" Brady asked. They didn't even bother to turn their heads to look at him, but continued pinpointing me.

"My partner asked you a question," I said flatly. Why is it that local cops have an instinctive dislike for state or federal agents? Partly it has to do with the arrogance that goes with working at the so-called upper level, the attitude that, as Lieutenant Mulvaney once put it, "Their shit don't smell." But mostly it has to do with their power to assume jurisdiction over a case you've worked on like a dog, and wrapping it up without saying a word about your contribution. Whatever it was it was there with these two guys, and I was in no mood to put up with their line of crap.

They looked at each other, and you could tell that the CIA guy had the final word on everything, that the FBI was along as a gofer. The FBI was needed because theoretically the CIA had no jurisdiction over domestic matters. But they didn't like each other separately as much as we didn't like them together, so there had to be somebody pretty big using them as a team.

"I can't give you any details," said Frye, "because national security is involved, but I can assure you that Miss Wade is indeed in good health, and is being looked after. We hope that in the near future she will

THE BROKEN-HEARTED DETECTIVE

be reunited with you, and this whole thing will be behind her."

"That's not enough," I told him. "You guys wrap national security around a pound of sausage, and think that nobody is supposed to ask what kind of garbage is ground into the mix. We don't buy that. There is no way this lady can be involved in any government hijinks of any kind. This whole thing stinks to the ceiling, and we're not going anywhere until she goes with us."

"Listen," said the CIA guy, "you two are in way over your heads, and you could drown in the soup. We're trying to keep this on a friendly basis, but if you push us, you could end up in custody at the least and with long prison terms a possibility. Back off before some real damage is done."

"Gee," said Brady, "you guys scare the hell out of us. You must have been real terrors in the Persian Gulf. Just remember that this is still the fucking United States of America, and we are guilty of no crime, and a young lady has seemingly been kidnapped, and you two are possible perpetrators. I've got a good mind to take your guns and badges and not give them back until your bosses come and say pretty please. You want to tango? You've come to the right ballroom."

They thought about it. They weren't what they were without being tough and disciplined and ready to do whatever the job required. But Brady gets that look on his face when he smells the battle coming on, and they knew that even if he was alone, there was a question of whether the two of them could take him. But there was also me, and although my heart was bunged,

37

I still looked real good on the outside, and together we definitely had them outmanned.

"Look, Altobelli," said the CIA guy, having made some kind of a decision, "you stay in this room tonight, and Miss Wade will call to assure you of her safety and good health. We are willing to do this because the stakes are so high that we can't afford to have you and your friend bumbling around the countryside making a stink. And we are also sympathetic to your concern over her welfare. We are both family men and can appreciate what you are going through. But I assure you that Miss Wade is under government protection and in no danger. I appeal to you as an American citizen who wants to do what's best for his country. And this is a matter of the utmost importance. Will you just give us until tonight?"

I looked over at Brady, and his look back indicated that whatever I decided he would go along with, whether it be taking these two apart or waiting for the call. I knew we couldn't make these two tell us what was going down no matter what we might do to them, and there was no sense in giving the authorities a valid reason for arresting us. The best thing would be to play it cool for the time being. At least we were ahead of where we had started from, and each step forward was one closer to Betty.

"What time will she be calling?" I asked.

"It will take a few hours to set this up," said Frye. "You should be getting the call somewhere around ten P.M."

"You understand," I said, "that this means nothing as far as getting her back is concerned. We don't leave here until she goes with us, and I don't give a goddamn what happens to national security or whatever other bullshit is involved in this. Betty Wade can in no way be involved in some kind of plot against the United States. This has all got to do with the guy who was in the hospital, and if we have to, we'll get to him eventually and see what he has to tell us."

"I assure you," said the FBI agent, "that Miss Wade is an innocent party in all this, and she is being secluded for her own protection. We want just as much as you do to have her free and back in her regular life."

"No you don't," said Brady. "Take a look at Vinnie's face. If you guys knew him the way I do, you'd make a call now and have her on her way before he gets really upset. I don't give a shit if you've got the whole military machine geared against us, Vinnie's gonna get his girl back."

The two of them looked into my face as though they were trying to find the secret of life, but I just stared back at them. That goddamned Brady was becoming quite an orator. I was glad he was on my side. I was glad he was my friend. If it wouldn't have embarrassed him, I would have kissed him right on the lips the way my uncle Pietro does because he's so grateful to be part of the family.

"You'll be hearing from her tonight," said Frye, and they were gone.

Brady waited a minute and then opened the door a crack to see if they might be listening at the door. The hall was empty.

"You know what, Vinnie?" he said. "I'm beginning to think there is more to this than meets the eye."

7

Brady wanted to go out to dinner because he hated room service food, and I felt we should stay right there in case the call came through early. We compromised by going to the hotel dining room, and me telling the switchboard operator where I could be reached.

"The guy said it was going to take some time, Vinnie," said Brady as we sat down at our table, "and you'd go nuts just staring at the TV screen."

"We can't afford to screw up on anything," I told him. "Who knows how many players are in this game? I was worried before, but now I'm scared stiff."

"I've got to admit that those feds sure surprised the hell out of me," admitted Brady. "It's hard to figure how your girlfriend got caught up in the middle of a bunch like that."

"It's that mystery son of a bitch," I said. "That could be the only explanation."

"Are we eating on Pardo money?" Brady asked as the waiter came up.

I nodded that we were, and he went crazy with shrimp cocktail, sirloin strip, baked potato, fresh asparagus and Caesar salad, all the things that cops eat when somebody else is picking up the tab. I had poached salmon, rice and a salad with oil and vinegar,

THE BROKEN-HEARTED DETECTIVE

and I only played with the food while Brady slogged his way through everything he ordered plus a full basket of rolls. For the first time I noticed that there was just the beginning of a pot belly starting to show in his middle. We used to work out together in the gym, but when I had to give it up, he started to slough off, and his pregnancy was now there for all to see. I still would have considered it an even bet if he was going against Mike Tyson, but I would have worried about the late rounds.

I finally couldn't stand it any longer and left while he was forking down apple pie a la mode. The switchboard lady said there had been no calls, and when I got back to the room, the little red light wasn't blinking on the phone. It was 7:30 and if the feds hadn't been lying, there were still a few hours to go.

Brady had been right about me staring at the TV screen so I switched it off and sat on the couch. If those feds had told the truth, at least Betty was alive, but I worried that she might get hurt before we could spring her. Admitting that I was in love was tough enough all by itself, but what if I never saw her again? And then the worst fear of all hit me. What if she didn't love me? What if after all was said and done, it turned out that she had only contacted me because she considered me a friend? Or that I owed her one for what she had done for me. What if she had only been trying to help me through a tough time, and that was all there was to it? No. She had called me specifically when she was in trouble, hadn't she? Had she called anybody else? Were there now a slew of guys in Tucson turning over the rocks in the desert in the hunt for Betty Wade?

There was a fumble at the door, and then Brady

came through it looking disgustedly at the card you had to stick in the slot to get it to open.

"You know what?" he asked. "I had half a beer left and didn't want to waste it. Beer and apple pie and ice cream go pretty well together." He had a look on his face like he had just discovered a new planet. "But goddamn," he continued, "that stuff goes through me like it was Niagara Falls."

He went into his bedroom to go to the john, but he was back before he would have had time to unzip.

"Vinnie," I heard him say in a strange voice, and I turned around to see him backing out of the bedroom with his hands in the air. Standing in front of him was a woman carrying one of those .22 calibers with a silencer screwed into the barrel, and the muzzle was pointed straight at the middle of Brady's bulging belly.

8

Scary as a gun is when it's pointed in your general direction and can explode at any second, my mind centered on the face of this incredible looking woman rather than the death she could deal out. After eleven years on the force, you automatically note statistics. She was maybe five feet, eight inches tall standing in what looked like cut-off combat boots, with the kind of slim build that has nothing to do with skinny, more like one of those saplings that will spring back and slash your face if you push it without thinking.

The features were interesting as well as beautiful. Her brown eyes were slightly almond-shaped, enough to tell you that she had some kind of Asian blood in her, and maybe two or even three kinds of Caucasian strains. But what got me most was the look on her face. There was no fear and no strain. She was holding a gun on a guy who was six feet, four inches tall with maybe two hundred and thirty-five pounds on him, and in the background was me, another fairly big man who could only be covered by shifting the angle of the gun away from her primary target, and she didn't shade a hair. You knew by looking at her that it would be no problem, physically, psychologically or morally, for her to pump a bullet into either of us if the situation demanded it.

"Back up to where you friend is," she instructed Brady, who took immediate action, "and both of you keep your hands where I can see them."

Brady had slipped off his holster and left it on the desk on his way to the bathroom, and my gun was on the coffee table in front of me. She moved around to where she had both of us covered, standing far enough away so that it would take three giant steps to get to her even if she said, "Yes, you may." You couldn't tell if she was a cop or not, but she'd had some professional training somewhere.

"Which one is Altobelli and which Brady?" she asked.

"He's Altobelli," said Brady, "and I'd like to put my hands down." She nodded permission.

"Why are you two looking for this nurse?" she asked. Brady looked at me.

"She's my fiancée," I told her.

"She wears no ring."

"We're not officially engaged. But we will be as soon as I find her."

"Who are you two? What are your backgrounds?"

"We're both former cops who live in San Bernardino," said Brady, "and we came out here to find Vinnie's girl. Are you with a government agency?"

Her mouth twisted into what could have been described as a smile, but there was something missing.

"You could say that," she answered. "Now I am going to go to the desk and the table and pick up the guns. Stand very clear with no sudden motions. Then I want both of you to carefully, most carefully, extract some identification and lay it on the table. Do it one at a time with Mr. Brady first."

Brady was standing at the end of the couch and had the best chance of getting at her, while I was hampered by having the heavy glass coffee table in front of me. Being Brady, he went for her no matter what the odds.

Only the edge of my right eye had caught the action, but her move had been such a blur that it took me a few seconds to piece together how it had gone down. As Brady had lunged, she had twisted into the air and both her feet had lashed out at him as she came round. And then, I swear, she had done a back flip and landed on her feet with the gun pointing at me. We had all kinds of guys on the force who were black belts in this or that, who looked like assholes as they hopped around the gym with their hands waving and their mouths emitting grunts and snarls that were supposed to terrify you. To my knowledge, no one had ever utilized this shit in making an arrest. Usually when push came to shove, they all pushed and shoved like the rest of us.

But she had done it; she was the real thing. She had taken out Brady, and as I looked down at him, one hand grabbing his chest, the other his stomach, I was happy to see that he was managing to suck air into his body. You want to know something terrible? At the back of my mind there was just the faintest bit of satisfaction at his being taken down by a girl. I was chasing a teenage punk up a flight of stairs when I had my heart attack, and I knew that although everybody wished me well, they all figured that this kind of thing would only happen to a wussy. Even Brady looked kind of funny whenever he mentioned it. Now he was lying on the rug gulping in great gasps of air while the woman who downed him was standing there with not a hair out of place. I couldn't help it.

"Lady," I said, "you are something."

She smiled. Not a big smile but enough to show that she appreciated the humor in someone like her outmanning Brady at the thing he did best.

"Would you put your identification on the table, and then move back six feet," she said. *Six feet.* She didn't want me to move five or seven feet. Six feet was what she had determined was the right distance for me to be ineffective if I decided to try a Brady death move on her. I moved back and watched as she came to the table and picked up my wallet. There was no foolishness about coming close enough for Brady to reach out a hand and pull her down to the floor with him. She sensed that even if he was dying, he would never give up, and I respected her respect for what he could do. He had already pushed himself up to a sitting position, but was still having trouble pulling breaths into his body. Guiltily I began to worry about how bad she might have hurt him.

She threw my wallet back on the table and let her gun hand fall to her side. It was a small gesture, but enough to show that she might believe we were telling the truth.

"Tell me about the nurse," she said.

You get hunches about people. Sometimes you're right and sometimes you're very, very wrong, but I had a good hunch here. It wasn't as good as the one with Bridget, but it was sufficient. So I told everything, starting with the message on my phone tape to our trip to Tucson to what we had learned from Bridget and the people at the hospital right down to the two government men who had paid us the visit. She would nod every once in a while to push me another step along the way until we reached the point where I said we were waiting for the call and that was as far as it had gone until she showed up.

Brady pushed himself to his feet, but he was a little bent over as he stood there. I couldn't tell from his face whether or not he approved of my letting this stranger know everything we knew, but at that point I didn't care. The other people had things to hide, but we didn't. I wanted the whole world to know that Betty Wade was missing, and we were looking for her. If silence would keep her from getting hurt, then that is what we would do, but if shouting would bring her back, then I would use the sound system of some heavy metal rock group.

When I finished, she stood there looking at me for a moment, and said, "My name is Daphne LaRocque, and I will help you if you will help me."

"Fuck you, lady," said Brady, and I thought for a moment he was going to take another try at her.

"Perhaps when you are feeling better," she suggested, and Brady, sick and embarrassed as he felt, worked up a little smile at that one.

"How can you help us?" I asked her.

"I can tell you about the man responsible for all this happening," she said, "and I will do what I can to get your fiancée back if you will help me kill him."

9

She caught me by surprise, but I didn't even blink.

"You've made me an offer I can't refuse," I told her.

What can you say when somebody makes a statement like that? Sorry, but it would be against Boy Scout regulations? Brady and I hadn't come to Tucson to take a life. We were there to save a life. Now this woman wanted to trade me Betty for us helping her zonk this guy. No matter what she had proposed I would have said yes. It wouldn't bother me one bit to promise her the moon and end up giving her a piece of cheese. There was no honor among any of the people we had met—doctors, hospital officials, nuts like the one who was threatening Betty, FBI, CIA, you-name-it—and I could play that game if I had to. And then I could walk away from that promise without even thinking that I had to go to confession. All I wanted was to get Betty Wade and take her back to San Bernardino safe and sound. So if this strange lady promised she would help us if we assisted her in offing the mystery man, she had our word on it. Maybe God would be annoyed with me for breaking that word, maybe he would send me straight to Hell, but if that was what it was going to take, that was what it was going to be.

Except that she wasn't any goddamned fool either.

"If we make this agreement," she said, "you had better keep your end of the bargain. Happy endings can be temporary. You don't know me and I don't know you, but let me assure you that both my experience and ability are such that it would not pay to try to cheat on any contract we make."

Contract. She had used the word *contract.*

"We're not killers," I told her, "but if this man is responsible for the danger Betty is in, then I will do what is necessary to make her life safe and him incapable of hurting her."

"He must be made incapable of hurting anyone ever again," she said, her voice flat like a judge pronouncing a sentence. "He has done enough damage to the world."

"Who the Christ is he, lady?" asked Brady, and I was gratified to hear that his voice had some strength in it. One hand was still giving light rubs to his solar plexus, but the other one was off his chest. He seemed all right but at the same time he seemed different. He was maybe still trying to figure out what it felt like to be taken down by a woman. Nobody, neither man nor beast, had ever taken Brady down in his whole life, and you could tell that this experience was still one that didn't have a file name on it. The Irish don't have as many macho problems as us Italians, but Brady was a breed unto himself. You could tell he wasn't planning at that moment how he was going to avenge his humiliation. But some time in the near future she was scheduled to be down on her back with Brady's foot on her throat.

"Why don't we all sit?" she suggested, leading the way by perching on the edge of a chair. We were all going to be buddies once she explained the situation, but she still had both her gun and ours conveniently near. So we sat.

"The man who is after your woman," she began, "is named Kurt Reich." No native-born American would have used the word *woman* the way she had. Although her English was perfect, she had definitely not grown up in this country. "Reich," she continued, "was a high official in your Central Intelligence Agency. (*Your.* She had said *your.*) A very high official. He was not in the regular chain of command and reported only to Director Casey, nobody else. Oliver North was an errand boy compared to Kurt Reich."

The man who is after your woman, she had said. The government guys had claimed that Betty was under their *protection.* Did this mystery lady even know about the feds? At the least, she wasn't in with them, and at the most who was she in with? Was she some kind of decoy that this guy Reich, if that was his name, had sent to us?

"Kurt was an integral part of every major CIA operation that occurred in the past twenty-five years," she continued. "Iran-Contra was his in both inception and execution. But when the director died, Kurt was forced out. They probably planned to kill him, but he was smarter than all of them put together. He informed Reagan and afterward Bush that he had tapes and videos and memos that revealed everything about everybody, and if anything happened to him, all the material would be released to the news media. They told him he was bluffing so he let them see a copy of one of the videos, and his battle was immediately won. If this material was released to the public, the country would be shaken to its very roots, and some very highly placed officials and former officials would end up completely disgraced or even in prison. History would have to be rewritten."

"But that was Reagan and Bush," said Brady. "Clinton wouldn't give a rat's ass if they had the stick shoved up them."

"Clinton can't afford any more negative news about the CIA after what's happened this past year," she replied. "He is not about to rock the boat."

"How do you know all this?" asked Brady.

She thought about it for a few seconds before she answered.

"I worked for Reich for many years," she answered. "Many, many years. He was my trainer, my master. He was my whole world."

And then I got it.

"Until he told you to take a hike," I said.

She sat there like she was carved in stone.

Brady was quicker than I was this time.

"You're the one who knifed him," he said.

Her silence was her answer.

"But why would these government guys claim they have Betty?" I asked. I couldn't have cared less that this Daphne was the one who had knifed the creep.

THE BROKEN-HEARTED DETECTIVE

Another inch and Betty wouldn't be going through all this.

She thought about this.

"They know Kurt wants her," she concluded, "and they're holding her in case they need her as bait."

"But if the government guys are the ones protecting him," said Brady, "why would they work against him?"

"Their goal is to find out where the incriminating evidence is hidden," she said. "Once they neutralize that, then Kurt is a dead man."

"So how can he allow them to be his bodyguards?" asked Brady. "It doesn't make sense."

"They aren't the real bodyguards," she said. "He uses them as errand boys. Kurt made millions in drug money during Iran-Contra. He has his own force of bodyguards that he pays himself, and they are the only ones he allows near him. These are all former CIA men who used to work for him and were discarded by the company. They know their whole future depends on him, and they guard him with their lives. It was only because they didn't know Kurt planned to banish me that I was allowed to stay near him. He wasn't able to shout with the knife in him, or I would have been killed on the spot."

"So they're looking for you too?" asked Brady.

"Yes," she answered, "and if they get me, I am dead."

"How come he's staying at this resort?" asked Brady.

"It is a perfect hiding place right out in the open," said the woman. "There are all those hundreds of guests there. Kurt has the presidential suite, which is in a separate building and quite defensible. If the government did decide to take Kurt out, they would have to lure him away from the resort. A frontal assault would be deadly, and nothing could be done secretly with all those people around. The media would be on it like flies on carrion."

"But if the government can't do anything, what the hell can we do?" asked Brady. "You're pretty goddamned good, lady, and we're not so bad ourselves, but from what you're saying it would take an infantry battalion with tank support to overrun the position, and all we've got is us and a rented Cadillac convertible."

"I have accomplished the impossible before," she said, "and I can do it again. There is always a way, and it will eventually come to me. It may take a very elaborate plan, or perhaps some window of opportunity for which we must perpetually be ready. But it will come and I will do it, alone if necessary, but more likely with your help."

"Suppose, just suppose," I said, "that these government guys really have Betty and that we could take her away from them and get her out of here. Would she be safe if we took her back to California? Would that be the end of it? What would happen then?"

"Kurt would come after her," said the woman, her voice showing that she believed it completely. "Once he has had her, he may just toss her aside. But until then, he will never stop. Since he left the service, this is the only game he has to play. All that talent and experience are churning inside him all the time, and he has no other outlet. There is only the excitement of the chase, and the satisfaction of the kill."

"This guy sounds creepy, lady," said Brady. "Why the hell did you hook up with him in the first place, and why did you stay with him once you knew what the score was?"

The look on her face was a little bit frightening, the eyes narrowing, the lips tightening, her whole body like a piano wire.

"He's the most fascinating man I ever met," she said. "The excitement of being with him was almost more than I could stand. Once it happened, I knew that there could never be another man or another way of life for me."

"But you want to kill him," said Brady. "You just said you wanted to kill him."

"If I cannot have him, he cannot live," she said, her voice rising to a sharp pitch. "He does not want me anymore, and he will not change his mind. That is why he must die."

"Are you crazy?" I asked her.

She considered the question seriously.

"Yes," she said, "I suppose I could be classified as crazy. But basically the world is crazy, is it not? I am just carrying things a few steps beyond ordinary."

"If you are crazy," I said, "how do we know we can count on you to help us get Betty back?"

"If you are sane," she answered, "how do I know you will help me kill Kurt?"

The phone rang. The clock radio showed it was ten P.M. Right on the button government style. I looked at the woman as I stood up to answer the phone. Crazy or not, if she could help us get Betty back, I was ready to go crazy too. Still crazy, I thought, still crazy after all these years.

10

"Altobelli," I said into the receiver.

"Hold," said a voice and I couldn't tell whether it was that of either of our afternoon visitors. I was holding all right, the knuckles on my hand almost pure white.

"Altobelli?" asked a woman's voice.

It wasn't her voice as I remembered it, and a howl almost went out of me as I realized how afraid she must be to speak in such a light whisper.

"Betty," I said, "don't be afraid. Brady and I are here to bring you home."

"I am all right," she recited. "They are taking good care of me, and if you go back to San Bernardino, I will be home with you soon."

"Okay," I yelled. "Whoever is monitoring this phone had better get Frye on it at once. I want to talk to Frye. Not Yert. Frye!"

There was silence for about twenty seconds, and then a voice said, "Frye here." It was the right voice.

"Listen, you son of a bitch," I told him. "I don't know what you've threatened her with, but you better get her to this hotel room as soon as possible, and then we're taking her out of here. Do you read me?"

"You're the one who better read me, mister," he

THE BROKEN-HEARTED DETECTIVE

said. "We'll do what we want when we want to, and you're the one who better keep his mouth shut and leave town before something happens that you'll regret for the rest of your life."

"Frye," I said, and I tried to keep my voice as even and hard as Mel Gibson did in the *Lethal Weapon* movies. "We know about Reich, we know about the tapes and the videos and all that crap, and we have made arrangements for the shit to hit the fan if something happens to us or she isn't brought here immediately."

He drew in his breath so hard that it sounded like a wind breaking loose before a storm. Then there was a silence.

"I can't do that," he finally said. "I can't do any of that without clearance. You'll have to give me some time."

"Let me put it this way," I told him. "If I don't get to see her in person before the night is out, we're going to blow the whole thing, including the fact that you're holding this girl a prisoner."

There was another silence.

"Look," he said, "if we bring you out to see her and we explain the circumstances, will you hold everything as it is?"

"How long will it take to bring me to her?"

"We can't do it before morning. We'll get you at first light. Zero six hundred hours. We'll get you at zero six hundred hours. We'll come and get you and Brady."

"No," I told him, "just me. Brady stays where he is. And it isn't just me and Brady who have the material. There are two other parties involved now."

"Who are they?"

55

"Jesus Christ, Frye," I said, "let's get real here. I want to see her tonight."

"No, we really can't do that. I've got to talk to people in Washington who might not be reachable. Tomorrow morning. I promise you you'll see her tomorrow morning."

"We are serious, Frye, deadly serious. You could be the one to fuck it up for the whole government. Think about that. Think about your future, Frye. Now put Betty back on."

There was a pause and then I heard her again.

"Altobelli?"

"I'm coming to see you in the morning," I told her. "Everything is going to be all right. You can ease up. Try and get some sleep. Just remember that I'll be there in the morning."

"Altobelli," she said, "don't overdo. Are you taking your pills?"

"Like a clock," I told her.

"It's so good to hear you. I'll see you in the morning. They say I have to get off now."

"I'll be there, Betty. I'll be there in the morning."

There was a click and then the buzz tone. And then another click. Our line was tapped. And by people who weren't very skilled at it.

When I hung up, I put my finger to my lips and made the shush signal.

"Your line is bugged," said Daphne, "but the room is clean. I checked it. What happened?"

I told the two of them what they hadn't figured out from hearing my end of the conversation.

"They've got her out in the desert somewhere," said Daphne. "They'll let you see her, but they won't give her up. If need be, they're going to use her to try to pull Kurt out in the open or to find out where the tapes are hidden. How would you feel about all the stuff he has being released to the media? Would it bother you if some of the top people in the country are disgraced?"

"It might be our only chance to clean out the politicians once and for all," said Brady, and I was able to match his smile. I felt better now that I had heard her voice. We had a long way to go, but the heaviness was lifting from my belly.

"Okay then," said Daphne. "We go for it. I have to get out of here and start things rolling. I'll be in touch with you."

"How can we reach you if we need to?" asked Brady.

"You can't," she answered. "I'll be contacting you. Now you have to go out in the hall and pull the emergency fire alarm."

"What?"

"They've got you under surveillance. We have to get a lot of people milling around out there if they're not going to spot me. Getting in was one thing, getting out is another."

When Brady went out to the hall to get things rolling, Daphne stuck her hand out at me and said, "So we've got a deal, have we?"

"Lady," I told her, reaching over and shaking like it was a Kiwanis meeting, "after seeing you perform, I don't want to be on any other side."

Right then Brady pulled the lever in the hall that started a fire drill that took a good hour for the officials to sort out and allow everybody back in their rooms. We walked down the stairs to the lobby with all the people on our floor, some of whom might have been there to watch us, and we waited there till the all clear sounded.

"What do you think of the broad?" Brady asked.

"What?"

"That Daphne? What do you think of her?"

"She knocked you on your ass, didn't she?"

"Two out of three," said Brady. "Two out of three."

When we got back to the rooms, Daphne was gone. I set the alarm for five-thirty, called the operator and left a five-thirty wake-up call because I never trusted hotel clock radios, undressed and got in bed. Then I slid out again, put on the light and went into the bathroom.

"What are you doing?" Brady called from his room.

"Betty told me to take my pills," I said.

It sure felt good to be under my nurse's care again.

11

They were thirty-five minutes late. I had been fifteen minutes early so that meant standing out in the freezing desert cold for forty-five minutes without having had coffee and my mouth beginning to sour the sweetness of the toothpaste.

I had slept in maybe twenty-minute snatches, my eyes continually springing open to check the time on the clock. At twenty-four minutes past three, Brady had called out, "What time is it?" and I told him.

"You sleeping at all?" he asked.

"Not much."

"Me neither, and she's not even my girl."

The wave of love that went over me brought tears to my eyes. Italians are very emotional people to begin with, but to have a friend like Brady by your side was a gift from God. I had brought him five hundred miles from home into a situation that could go deadly wrong, and he wasn't sleeping because he was upset that I wasn't sleeping.

He was snoring away when I got up to go, however, so I tiptoed through everything until I was out the door. As I walked down the hall to the elevator, I wondered if somebody in one of the rooms was signaling somebody else that Altobelli was on his way. But then they let me stand there for forty-five minutes in the morning chill. If this was their idea of psychological warfare, they were fooling with the wrong psycho.

There were three of them in the car, two in front and one in back, but Frye and Yert weren't among them. Big guys, all of them, maybe from a muscle squad. As we pulled away from the curb, the one beside me asked, "Are you carrying?"

"I left it up in the room."

"I've got to check anyway," he said, running his hands all over my body, including ankles, crotch and small of the back. "He's clean," he told his buddies.

We drove out of the city toward the east, but as soon as we cleared buildings, they told me I had to put on a blindfold. There was no point in arguing so I sat for something like two hours while they twisted and turned and drove this way and that to confuse me. I wasn't even trying to make connections so I just let my body slump against the seat, and I think I dozed some of the time. I was definitely asleep when we stopped with a jerk that threw me forward. I heard the front door open on the passenger side, and the guy was out and back in about two minutes. From the creaking, I figured we had gone through a gate. Then we rode for what seemed like forever over a road so bumpy that my head hit the ceiling once, and the guy sitting next to me cursed the ability of the driver.

When we finally stopped, the blindfold was pulled off, and the door was opened for me to get out. We were in the middle of the desert somewhere, parked in the driveway of a long, one-story, adobe ranch house with what looked like barns on either side of it. There was scrub oak and cactus all around, but basically it was sand covered with rocks and boulders. I wondered how many of these guys had been in the deserts of the Persian Gulf. Probably none.

Frye and Yert and one other guy came out of the house to meet us. The sun was pouring down by then, and they had their jackets off so that their guns were right out in the open. Frye looked at the man who had been sitting next to me on the trip.

"He's clean," the guy said.

"I wish you wouldn't put us through all this," said Frye. "We explained to you that this is of the utmost national importance, and you are still causing us to divert our attention from the main problem. Once you have visited with Miss Wade, we expect you to go home and wait for us to clear up the situation."

I didn't bother to answer. He waited for a few seconds, sighed and then turned toward the house. When he realized I wasn't following, he stopped and turned around.

"She's in there," he said, pointing at the door.

THE BROKEN-HEARTED DETECTIVE

"I want to see her out here," I told him.

"You can't do that."

"Let's cut the crap," I told him. "Brady and our associates are waiting to hear from me by a specified time. If they don't or if anything happens to anybody, or anybody disappears, you're going to have the *Los Angeles Times* and Peter Jennings and Connie Chung and the "Today Show" and CNN calling to find out what the hell's the story on this guy Reich and the CIA connection. So don't try to bullshit me into playing your game. I'm going to lay down some rules too. I want to see her outside and I want to see her without any of you people standing close enough to hear. If that isn't good enough, then let's get in the car and go back to Tucson. Or shoot me down and bury me in the lone prairie. But those are my minimum conditions, and I'm getting impatient to see my fiancée."

"We don't shoot anybody down," said Yert loudly. "Christ, this is still the United States, and we are just trying to do our jobs. The situation is bad enough without you adding to it. Your fiancée is under government protection, and what we are trying to do is prevent her from being harmed or kidnapped. Because of you, we may not be able to do that, and it will be your responsibility if things go wrong. Now why don't you just talk to her, and then go back to Tucson and get your friend and return to San Bernardino? Your records indicate that you and your friend were exemplary police officers, and it would be a shame if you did anything to damage the interests of your country."

"Just bring her out here," I told him.

He looked at me for maybe twenty seconds, turned on his heel and went into the house. In a few minutes he led Betty out and brought her maybe two paces from me. She looked thin and tired and more beautiful than I remembered even though I had studied her face every second she had been my nurse in coronary care. When she smiled, it was almost as though she had to crack her lips to do it, and a surge of anger went through me then that made everything look hazy.

"Altobelli," she said, and the smile broadened. "I told you I was coming out here for a change of pace, but this is ridiculous."

I moved the two steps and put my arms around her, and she stiffened for a moment before relaxing into my body. It suddenly hit me. She didn't know she was my fiancée; she didn't know that I had been brooding about her ever since she had left San Bernardino. I was the cop who was her friend and she had called me as a friend. I had to get her alone before Yert wondered what was going on. I dropped my arms and turned to him.

"I'm going to take her out there," I said, pointing to an open space just past the house, "and we're going to talk so that I can check out what you've told me. After that, we'll see what happens."

He didn't protest at all, just moved aside so we could walk by him. We went maybe four hundred feet into the rocky sand, and when I turned to check on Yert, I saw that several more men had come out of the barns, and were moving to form a big circle around us. From the sky it must have looked like the fox and geese game we played when we were kids.

"Look," I told her, "these people think you are my fiancée. It was the only way I could convince them that I would never quit on getting you safe and home. We're in the middle of a pretty big deal, and it's going to take some doing to square it away, but eventually

THE BROKEN-HEARTED DETECTIVE

everything is going to be fine. You just have to be patient and give me some time."

"Altobelli," she said, "what are you doing out here? I just wanted your advice. My message said that I needed advice. You shouldn't be going through all this. I couldn't believe it when they told me you wanted to talk to me on the phone."

"The tape ran out on my answering machine, and I didn't get your whole message," I said. "But I would have come anyway. You mean more to me than anybody else in the world. Without you I've got nothing."

"You don't owe me anything, Altobelli. You barely know me. I'm attracted to you, but when I took you to bed it was out of friendship and caring. I was just showing you that your life had so much ahead of it despite your heart attack. You don't owe me anything. I appreciate your coming out here, but if anything happened to you, I would never forgive myself. These men have convinced me that they are holding me only for my own protection. They're government agents. They wouldn't do anything to hurt me."

Her words were not the ones I had journeyed to hear. She had been so much on my mind that I had come to believe she felt the same way I did. And when I was the one she called in her trouble, it had made it seem definite. She had taken care of me in the hospital because that was her job, and she had taken me into her bed because she wanted to prove to me that my life wasn't over. She liked me and that was as far as it went. But she had called *me!* I was the one she had called. So maybe she didn't yet feel the same way I did, but there was something special there that just needed time. Once we were clear of this mess I could show her how much love

I wanted to give her, and maybe she would feel it herself. But first I had to convince her of how much danger she was in.

"Do you know who the man is who gave you so much trouble?" I asked.

She shook her head, and I could see the fear there.

"His name is Kurt Reich," I told her, "and he's powerful enough so that even the U.S. government is afraid of him. He's a former CIA bigwig who knows where all the bodies are buried, and if they have to, they'll sacrifice anybody to get him. Or even worse, they'll turn you over to him to buy themselves some time. I know this is scaring the hell out of you, but you must realize that you can't trust these people, that we've got to get you away to where he can't bother you."

"What can you do that these people can't?" she asked.

"With us you know that you come first, ahead of anybody and anything. And Brady and I don't have to worry about the guy spilling government secrets. If some politicians take a fall over this, that's their problem. If we can get proof of whatever the hell he knows, then we can use that to blow the whistle on all of them."

"But wouldn't that be hurting our government?"

"I don't care who it hurts as long as it isn't you."

She reached up and put her hands on my shoulders, and there was a look on her face that reminded me of the night we made love.

"You know, Altobelli," she said, "I've got a feeling you didn't look on me as a one-night stand. Are you thinking of making an honorable woman out of me?"

"I'll give it to you straight," I told her. "Once we

THE BROKEN-HEARTED DETECTIVE

get clear of this I want us to get married. I have been thinking of nothing but you, and I never want to think of anybody but you. You gave me life, and now I want us to live it."

"We'll see, Altobelli," she said. "Now you've given me something to think about. In a way it scares the hell out of me that I was so important that you dropped everything and came out here after me all by yourself."

"Brady's with me," I said.

"Brady?"

"You met him. My partner. He retired from the force and now we have a detective agency."

She was staring at me, all mixed up.

"You're our first case," I told her. "Except that this one is for free because we're practicing."

She narrowed her eyes, not sure whether I was kidding or not.

"Altobelli," she said, "you're nuts enough to be my husband. But I want you to promise that you'll do nothing that will put you in danger or will strain your heart."

"I promise," I said. I was getting pretty good at lying.

"I want to get out of here and somewhere away from that creep so bad that I'll do what you say," she promised. "What do you want me to do?"

"You just sit tight while we do our thing," I told her. "For the time being, you're safer with these guys than you would be on your own or even with me. Brady and I will figure out a way to neutralize him, and then all the pressure will be off. But you get yourself some rest and eat regular so that you'll be ready for anything when the time comes."

"Hey," she said, tucking her arm into mine and turning me toward where Frye was standing, "you're my man."

We walked back to the circle of men.

"I want to take her with me," I told Frye.

"You know we can't do that," he answered.

"If you're thinking of using her as bait," I told him, "then we've got a personal thing between us."

"We don't use people as bait," he said. "We're keeping her strictly for her protection. And she'd be better off if you went back to San Bernardino and waited for us to clear things up."

"I might do that," I said. "I just might do that." Lying was getting too easy. He gave me a look that showed he wasn't a fool.

"They're going to take you back now," he said. "We'll be in touch."

I turned to look at Betty, and she came right into my arms, holding me tight against her.

"I'm going to kiss my fiancé good-bye," she said. "Would you have the decency to turn your heads?" All sixteen turned like one guy.

She moved her hand up to the back of my neck and pulled, and as I felt my lips mesh into hers, it was like we were back in bed again, her body into my body, her rhythm my rhythm. When she pulled her head away, there were tears in her eyes even though she was smiling.

"You know what, Altobelli?" she said. "You may be even smarter than I thought."

12

They removed the blindfold when we reached the outskirts of Tucson, and it was noon on the button when they dropped me in front of the hotel. There were no fond farewells exchanged, and I went right up to the room where Brady was sitting in front of the television set watching a rerun of "Beverly Hillbillies."

"How'd it go?" he asked.

"Have they had a chance to bug this room yet?" I wanted to know.

"They don't fill me in on these things."

"Why don't we have an early lunch?" I suggested.

We ended up in a diner that had four booths and maybe twenty stools, and sat where we could check everybody coming in. The booth farthest from us had two ladies in it, and there were seven people scattered on the stools. Brady ordered the meat loaf and mashed potatoes with gravy, and I asked for a tuna salad plate, which came with the most tired looking quarters of hard-boiled egg I had ever seen. I don't think they were from the same egg either because there were different shades of black around the yolks.

"How did it go?" Brady asked again.

Just then two guys came in and sat down in the very next booth to us. It couldn't have been clearer if they wore T-shirts with "Federal Dick" printed on both sides. We ate our meal in silence, paid and left. They had ordered only coffee, probably because of restrictions imposed by the size of the federal deficit, so it wasn't a big deal for them to wait a little bit and then come after us.

"Do we lose them, bruise them or schmooze them?" Brady wanted to know.

"Let's find a spot where they can't come too near," I suggested. "At least we know who these are, and maybe the backup team will stay out of sight."

"Do you figure the government can still afford backup teams?" Brady asked.

"I think maybe the drug people are being skimped because of this operation," I said. "This is one high-priority caper. They had twenty guys altogether out in the desert. Let's go sit on that single bench in the square there by the statue."

Without even discussing it, we put our hands in front of our mouths in case they had boomer microphones pointed at us.

"They drove me around blindfolded for two hours," I began, and then told him everything that had happened.

"Do you think we could spring her out of there if we found the place?" he wanted to know.

"I think the CIA guy's right about her being safer under their protection right now," I said. "Reich obviously doesn't quit on anything he wants. They seemed scared stiff of him. If just the two of us had her, it sounds like he could snatch her away easily, and he would probably track us down wherever we ran. I feel she's okay now, but the thing that worries me is that the government guys might use her for some sort of bait. No matter what they say, she's possible bait. We are too. Right now they're not sure how much we know and how much we've told unknown people so they'll move carefully. But once they decide on a course of action, they'll do what they think they have to do, and we'll all be what's known as expendable."

"So where do we go from here?" asked Brady.

"I was thinking about it all the way back to the hotel. There's nothing like a blindfold to help you concentrate. As long as we're out here, why don't we take a vacation at the Venture Canyon resort. Catch some rays, play some golf, swim in the pool and eat the good food. Money is no object, of course. And we just might get a better idea of who this guy is, and what we can do to put him out of the picture. He's got Betty scared stiff, and that's a real no-no."

"She sure must have been glad to see you."

"Yeah."

I considered telling him that her feelings for me didn't match mine for her, but didn't know how to word it. Brady was all vinegared up because we were there to rescue my woman, and it would take some of the bite out if he discovered she just thought I was a nice guy. It gave me a strange feeling to think about it. What if we got her free, and she said thank you and disappeared out of my life?

But the kiss she had given me, the good-bye kiss, that wasn't just a thanks-for-helping-me, see-you-around kind of kiss. Christ, I'd kissed and been kissed by enough women to know the difference. It was even different from the time we had gone to bed. Those had been loving kisses maybe but not love. Maybe the added oomph was because she was so grateful to find somebody trying to help her, but it hadn't felt like that. I thought about a future without her, and I didn't like what I saw. It was going to work out. Everything was going to work out.

"So what's our next move?" asked Brady.

"We check out of the hotel and get a room at Venture Canyon."

"What about our Indian trackers?" he asked, pointing at them standing on the other side of a flower bed near the park fence. They knew we'd made them, and they weren't making any pretense about not staring at us.

"Do you think that Cadillac's got enough juice to lose them?" I asked.

His face lit up like that of my three-year-old niece Philomena when you gave her a piece of chocolate. I had trouble keeping up with him on our walk back to the hotel, and when I got up to our room after paying the bill, he had packed not only his bag but mine too. We took the elevator straight down to the garage, waited while the guy located our vehicle, and were hitting nearly fifty when we came out on the street.

"Alive," I said to him, as he gave heart failure to a couple who were crossing the street with the usual indifference of the elderly. "It is imperative we get there alive."

"Where do you get all those big words and fancy talk?" he asked as he went between two cars who didn't know they had space between them.

"Carlotta," I explained. "She was as tough on me as she was on her students. She gave me a list every week, and if I screwed up, she threatened to withhold her body."

THE BROKEN-HEARTED DETECTIVE

"You're kidding. She really did that?"

"She tried, but she wanted it even more than I did, so I usually got by with a B average."

"She was some pistol. I was worried you were going to marry her. Do you ever see her?"

"She moved away a year after we broke up."

As we were talking, Brady was zooming around corners, and once he even went the wrong way down a one-way street. I kept waiting for the sound of a siren behind us, but we were lucky.

"Where the hell are we?" he asked.

I pulled the Arizona map from the glove compartment and turned to the side with the blowup of Tucson.

"As soon as we spot a sign that tells us what highway we're on, we'll know," I told him.

Around the very next curve was a marker saying we were on Route 86, but that didn't help until we stopped at a gas station, and the guy showed what roads to take to get to Venture Canyon. We had a cold drink while waiting to see if any chase cars showed up on the horizon, but only an Andretti could have followed Brady out of the city.

So there we were an hour later driving through the fancy gate of the Venture Canyon resort and up the winding road that had grass growing on both sides of it, which must have used up quite a bit of water each day. There were six young men waiting to unload our two small bags, and there were three young men behind the reception desk that had nobody in front of it.

"Yes, sir," said the shiniest faced one.

"We want to rent a room."

"And the reservation is in the name of ... ?"

"We don't have a reservation."

The atmosphere immediately changed. It seemed that nobody came to Venture Canyon without a reservation.

"Luckily, sir," said the young man, "we've had a cancellation and can squeeze you in. Would you like a room with two doubles or one king-size bed?"

As he said this, he looked up at Brady and smirked. It took me a few seconds to sort it out. The son of a bitch thought we were gay. Luckily, Brady didn't make the connection, or that poor bastard would have found himself being hauled over the counter and out the door.

"We would each like a bedroom," I told him, trying to look macho, but I could see that he had made up his mind even if I booked a whole floor.

"A suite?"

"That would do."

"I have one available at three hundred and forty-five dollars a day at our off-season rate."

Luckily again, Brady had drifted off to look at something, or the price would have put him into a frenzy.

"That will do nicely."

"And how will you be paying for this, sir?"

"Cash."

"Cash?"

"Yes. Cash."

"May I have a credit card, sir, just for our records?"

I fished the plastic out of my wallet, and he put it through the machine they have for checking it out. No gongs rang. I think I had a five-thousand-dollar limit on it even though I had never gone more than eight or nine hundred dollars.

"Front," the clerk called out, and then looked fixedly at the two small bags that had been deposited behind us. He wasn't dead sure we were worthy of Venture Canyon. If they were this frosty during off season, I didn't want to be there when the real snowbirds arrived.

13

Brady whistled when he saw the suite.

"This is better than the one I had in Vegas that time," he said, and retold the story of his gambling trip from the beginning through a very long middle to an endless end. I'll say this for him though. He never added any new stuff. Each time it was narrated exactly as he had reported originally. The man had integrity as well as a keen eye.

"What's the plan?" he asked, still frowning from seeing me give the bellman five dollars for installing us and explaining how the air-conditioning worked. He would have gone really berserk if he had noticed that the kid put both our bags in one bedroom without asking which went where. It seemed that at Venture Canyon everybody knew a couple of gay caballeros when they saw them.

The plan. What was the plan? I had no plan.

"Maybe we should just drift around the place and

find out what's what and who's who," I improvised. "Let's go buy some swimsuits and T-shirts and look over the pool and the golf course, and see if we can locate Reich."

It turned out to be easier than I could have imagined. When we reached the golf course, a foursome was getting ready to tee off on the first hole, and the setup was so obvious that even a rookie would have figured it out. Three of the guys were wearing the kind of sport shirts that hang over your pants, which is the only way to cover up a gun in hot weather. The fourth guy had his shirt tucked in, and a little shiver went through me when I looked at him.

He fit the general description that Daphne had given us, but that was only the tip of the iceberg. Every once in a while you come across a guy who scares you without him doing a thing. Just by looking at him you know that God blinked and the Devil stared when he went through the production line. In my eleven years on the force I had met only two men who had done that to me. One was a Colombian drug dealer who had hacked a whole family to death—father, mother, four little kids—and the other was Tony Pardo, the Mafia boss with the Harvard education. Now this guy made it a hat trick.

When I looked at Brady, I saw that he had connected too, but I doubted his reaction was the same as mine. Brady's Vietnam buddies had told me that he was the only soldier they knew who enjoyed the war, that each time they went out "in country," as they called it, Brady got the same look on his face as when he went home with a bar girl. In all my years with him I had seen him lose it only twice, once with a pimp who had beaten to death a fourteen-year-old

THE BROKEN-HEARTED DETECTIVE

runaway who wouldn't "cooperate," and the other with a girl's boyfriend who had burned the eyeballs of her two-year-old son with the tip of his cigarette. He damaged us as well as them when we tried to pull him off those people because right then he couldn't tell the difference between friend and foe, but usually he was so calm and quiet in tough situations that you would think he was a group therapist instead of a cop.

Reich was good-looking, I had to admit that. Everything fit just right on his face, and if I hadn't been told, I would have thought him to be much younger than just under fifty. He didn't talk at all, just stepped up to the tee when it was his turn, and belted a good one down the fairway. They all had hand-pulled golf carts, and I was sure I could see the muzzle of an automatic weapon sticking out of one of them. Nobody seemed nervous about anything, but these guys were ready in case something did break. They moved off for their second shots.

"That our boy?" asked Brady.

"I would think so."

"He ain't going to be easy."

"We're going to need luck as well as brains and brawn."

"The brains are your responsibility. I've got the brawn and the luck of the Irish."

Brady always acted as though I was the smart one who had to tell him to come in out of the rain, and I think he almost believed it, but it put me at a disadvantage because it forced me to act like I knew what we were doing when it was the luck of the Italians that came to my rescue most of the time. One of my grandfather's brothers was Niccolo Machiavelli Altobelli, and he couldn't even spell his middle name, let

75

alone do dire deeds in the dark. The same for my cousin Benito. We weren't the kind of Italians that hid poison in their rings.

"As long as we know that Betty is safe," I said, "there's no hurry about anything. We can take our time to assess the situation and project a course of action."

"Jeez," said Brady, "you sound just like the lieutenant at a briefing. Except that she would always stick a couple or three *fucks* in there to show she was one of the boys."

The resort brochure told us that the place was spread over a hundred acres with "virgin groves of mesquite, squawbush and blue paloverde," whatever the hell that was. There were four hundred and fifty rooms and suites, five restaurants and lounges, twelve tennis courts, the golf course, two swimming pools, a health club and spa, and five miles of fitness trails. There was a presidential suite that went for fifteen hundred bucks a night in season, according to the rate sheet, and it had twenty-five hundred square feet of space on its two floors with four outside patios and rooms downstairs suitable for "servants or guards."

Following the resort map, we wandered over to the presidential suite, which was a separate building on the end of the hotel closest to the side of the mountain.

"Looks pretty defensible," said Brady, as we strolled to the front steps and stopped to chat a bit. Maybe five seconds later two guys drifted up to us from somewhere around the corner of the building.

"Anything we can do for you gentlemen?" asked the bigger of the two, although they were both plenty

THE BROKEN-HEARTED DETECTIVE

big. I wondered if they were government or Reich's personal bodyguards.

Looking as vague as I could, I said, "What?"

"Are you here for some specific reason?"

"Vacation," I told him.

"What?"

"We're here on vacation. We just checked in and we're looking at all the high spots on the map."

"This is a restricted area," the guy said. "It's closed to the general public."

"Why?" Brady asked. "It doesn't say anything like that on the map." He pointed to the spot with his finger.

"You'll have to check with the concierge on that," said the bodyguard. "I'm just telling you that you have to leave."

"Well," said Brady, and so help me he batted his eyes at them, "that doesn't sound very friendly."

"We're very friendly," said the big guy. "That's why we're telling you to leave before things get unfriendly."

Brady turned on his heel and went stalking off. I stayed long enough to see the two guards give each other those knowing smiles, and then I followed my partner, who had walked so fast that he was out of sight behind some bushes.

"Did you see that?" Brady asked as I came abreast. "They all think we're fags, man. If you ever breathe a word of this to anybody else, anybody at all, you're dead meat."

Here I was thinking I was so clever in noticing how the reception clerk and the bellboy had pegged us, and Brady had picked it up without even giving me a hint.

"What the hell is there about us that they should pin lilies on our lapels?" I asked.

"I've been thinking about it," said Brady, "and I figure that most of the guys who come here in pairs are that way. So what do we do to show them how wrong they are?"

It hit me then.

"Let's do nothing," I told him. "You saw how those guys looked through us. We couldn't have a better cover than that. We'll dance our way around here and they'll come to take us for granted like we were flower beds, and when the right time comes, we unzip our flies and show them what we're really like. Let's get over to the shop and buy some gaily colored bathing trunks."

"I can see you getting away with it permanently," said Brady, "but once the babes at the pool get a real look at my tool kit I'll be swamped. Then what do we do?"

"We'll have a tiff and you can swing the other way."

"Yeah," said Brady. "If my wife ever heard about it, and even this far away that woman can hear like a bird dog, she'd fix me good enough to be a guard in a Turkish harem."

"Let's go buy the swim trunks," I said, getting excited about the possibilities of our cover. We started down the path when Brady stopped dead and stared at me with a pained look on his face.

"What's the matter?" I almost yelled, looking everywhere.

"No kissing on the lips," he said, and took off again.

14

For dinner, Brady had shrimp cocktail, sirloin strip, baked potato, fresh asparagus and Caesar salad. We decided to eat in the Flying T Bar and Grill because the gourmet restaurant looked too dark, and the aroma of grilled beef practically pulled Brady by the nose into the restaurant where the waiters were dressed cowboy style, and they arrested anybody who didn't laugh uproariously.

It was a happy crowd, that was for sure. Most of the tables seemed to be occupied by couples who were at a convention of funeral directors. We figured it out from the jokes they were loudly telling each other. The women were drinking one for one with the men, and I figured there were going to be a lot of dead bodies lying around the rooms by midnight.

"Did you catch the corner table?" I asked Brady as the waiter went to fetch our beers.

"The seven guys?"

"They're all carrying."

Five of them had jackets on, and the other two were wearing the loose-fitting sports shirts that hung outside their pants. We had decided to strap our guns to our legs because these were pros we were dealing with, and they would have picked us out immediately if we had shoulder holsters under jackets or shirts. One of the guys was from the pair that had braced us near the presidential suite, and he said something to his buddies about us because they all looked over at once with big smiles on their faces. Brady and I took no notice as we sipped our beers, and I wondered what he would do if I reached over and squeezed his hand. The stakes were too big to fool around, but I was in a good mood because I knew Betty was alive and deep down I had a feeling that everything was going to work out all right.

"What's the next move?" asked Brady, as he sliced off a chunk of steak. I swirled some of the pasta primavera around my fork as I pondered the question.

"Somehow or other we've got to get close enough to this guy to find out where he's got the stuff the government wants," I said, "and then we've got to neutralize it."

"I don't want to sound like a killjoy," said Brady, "but we haven't got a chance in hell to break through his security. Those are all pros over there, and I've got a feeling the whole crew is well tuned. It could be that nothing's going to work for us here, and maybe we'll have to handle it from the other side. Find out where your girl is, grab her and run and hope that Reich will quit on it or the feds will do their thing before he can come after her."

"It could take us weeks to find where they've got her," I said, putting down the fork and staring at the pasta sauce turning into paste. "They could also keep moving her around. They've got more guys there than this guy has here. And after looking at him, I have the feeling he doesn't quit on anything." I didn't feel good. I didn't feel good at all. Nothing was working right.

"Hey," said Brady, "don't go Italian army on me. We just got here and maybe tomorrow or the day after we'll find a chink somewhere, and we'll chisel at it until we've got a hole big enough to crawl through. Do you think the deep-dish apple pie is any good here?"

"If you have it with ice cream," I told him.

15

One of the funeral wives dropped her steak knife on her foot, and since she was wearing open-toed sandals, the blade went deep enough to stand straight up, which brought forth one of the damndest screams anybody ever heard. The interesting thing was that the seven guys at the corner table immediately went into evasive action when they didn't know what the problem was, and one of them even pulled his gun right out in the open for a couple of seconds.

A stalwart soul at the victim's table yanked the knife out, which brought forth some blood, and the woman fainted dead away. The funeral directors bore her off in professional style to somewhere, maybe her room, and I'm sure the hotel had a doctor and a bunch of insurance forms to fill out quick as a bunny wherever they laid her out. One of the drunken ladies at the death table moaned very loudly, "She didn't even have a chance to eat her dessert," but the remaining ones were soon laughing as loudly as ever.

Brady wondered about maybe having a beer at the nightclub when we finished eating, but things caught up with me all of a sudden, and I felt tired to the point where I was almost shaky. It had been seven months since my heart attack, and I was feeling much stronger, but there was still a long way to go. Maybe too long. Both my doctor and Betty had counseled me to think positively, but whenever I thought about what it had been like to run full out until I got my second wind, or punch the big bag in the gym until the sweat blinded my eyes, or play football with my brothers on a Saturday morning, or take on some muscle-bound cokehead who thought he could beat up on the world, I got that bad feeling in the pit of my stomach. There was the temptation to go have a beer with Brady and screw it, but I wanted to live, to stay alive, to taste the good food and romp with my brothers' kids and hang with Brady and maybe, if God allowed it, have Betty Wade around for the rest of my life.

I reminded him that we had a minirefrigerator full of bottled goods in our suite, and even though he complained that the beer in the room cost double, he came along without any real fuss. He called his wife to tell her we would be a few more days, and I dialed my mother to give her approximately the same message. All of my four brothers had asked her where I was, so I gave her the address and the phone number because that would give them the impression I was on vacation with Brady. My brothers had always babied

THE BROKEN-HEARTED DETECTIVE

me because I was the youngest, but they worried even more now that I was a cardiac instead of a hard case.

Brady was drinking his beer and watching "Cheers," but I was too restless to sit still. There were two opposing armies out there, the feds and Reich's bunch, and we were two guys caught in the middle. There was now no doubt in my mind that the CIA would throw Betty to the wolf without even a second thought. The FBI guys might think twice about it because they didn't bullshit themselves into believing that they shaped the destiny of the entire world, but those guys followed orders to the letter too, and if Washington laid down a directive, they would follow it even if it meant sacrificing an innocent young woman. I looked down at my hands and they were clenched into fists.

My mind was so deep into thinking about Betty that Brady heard the knocking before I did. He switched off the set with the remote, hitched up his pants leg to check on his gun and walked over to the side of the door. I moved behind one of the tall chairs where I wouldn't be quickly noticed by anyone coming into the room.

"Yes?" said Brady.

"Hi," said a man's voice. "My name is Terry Bradley, and I would like to see you if I may."

"About what?" asked Brady.

"Well, it's rather personal."

Brady looked over at me and I nodded, stooping over so I could pull the gun out as quickly as possible. Brady stood to the side and tugged the door open with his left hand. A guy was standing there, a big guy, and when he came through the door, he looked so familiar that I thought I knew him from somewhere. I did. He was the Reich guard who had pulled his gun out when the woman had knifed herself in the steak house. That's what had burned his face into my mind. His hands were empty so I stood up.

Brady took a quick, careful look into the hall before he closed the door. He obviously hadn't spotted anybody because I could see his body relax as he walked to the center of the room and sat down again. Except that I realized he had sat so that his right hand was near his ankle gun. I moved over and stood beside the couch with a look on my face of what I hoped was polite interest.

"Hi," the guy said again. We smiled at him. He smiled back. Had Reich already made us, and this guy was there to warn us off? Or was he going to invite us somewhere, and then we would disappear? No matter what it was it couldn't be good.

"I saw you two at the pool today, and then I saw you again at the Flying T," he said. We smiled some more.

"Things are pretty lonely here right now," he said, "and I thought maybe we could get to know each other. There were a couple of swell guys here last week, but they had to go back to Minneapolis. So I thought maybe you two would like to have a couple of drinks, and maybe we could do something together."

Christ, the guy was gay! I looked over at Brady and saw that he hadn't made the connection yet. This gay thing was getting out of hand, but it hit me so hard that I almost stepped back a pace. This was one of the bodyguards. Who the hell knew what he might lead us to? He wanted a couple of new friends, by Jesus he was going to get a couple of new friends.

"Terry," I said, walking over to him with my hand

THE BROKEN-HEARTED DETECTIVE

outstretched, "I'm Vincent and this is Matthew. We're delighted to make your acquaintance." Don't lisp, I was telling myself. Whatever you do, don't lisp.

"Hi, Terry," said Brady, stretching out his hand for a shake but not getting up. He knew there was something different about this so he was being very, very careful.

"Please sit down," I said. "May I offer you a drink?"

"Scotch would be lovely," he answered. "On the rocks with just a bit of soda."

While I was busying myself at the minibar, Terry was looking around the suite.

"Very nice," he said. "They've got four of us cramped into one small room at our place."

"Are you here with the convention?" Brady asked.

"Oh my no," said Terry. "I'm one of Kurt Reich's assistants."

All that big deal of secrecy at the hospital, and at the resort he was registered under his own name. Curiouser and curiouser.

"Who is Mr. Reich?" I asked as I handed him his drink. "Is he with the resort? Do you work here?"

"Oh my no," he said. "Mr. Reich is an international financier who is vacationing here just like everybody else. He loves the desert so he rented the presidential suite for a few months."

"So that's who's in there," said Brady. "We were walking by there this afternoon minding our own business when two very rude men came out and told us we had to move on. Did they think we were robbers or something?"

"Oh, no," said Terry. "It's just that Kurt was nearly

kidnapped once in Italy, and he's been a bug on security ever since."

"Well," said Brady, "those men were needlessly rude."

"All those fed ... all those outside security guards are pains," said Terry. "We keep telling Kurt that the seven of us can handle his security without any trouble, but he likes to have a lot of people running around."

"Just like Elvis," I said.

Both Brady and Terry looked puzzled.

"He liked to have a lot of guards and gofers to keep him company," I explained.

"Oh, Kurt isn't like that at all," said Terry. "He's a very private man. I just joined up with him, and even though I'm his nephew, I barely get to see him."

"His nephew?" Brady said.

"Yes. My mother is his older sister, and she's been after him to teach me the business, and he finally said I could come here after I quit law school. But he says I have to act as though we're not related, and I've got no one to talk to."

Jesus! Was this guy for real? What kind of a trap was being set up for us? Brady and I looked at each other, and his eyebrows were almost an inch higher than normal.

"How many of you are there?" I asked.

"What?"

"You said you had no one to talk to, but you're in a room with three others, and there seem to be more than that."

"Oh, yes, there are fifteen of us altogether. But the fed ... but the outside guards all stick to themselves, and Uncle Kurt's permanent people barely look at me, let alone speak. This may sound strange to say, but they scare me."

"Scare you?" said Brady.

"Isn't that weird?" said Terry. "But you can't imagine what those people are like. They're not at all like us."

"Us?"

"Yes, you know. That's why I feel so alone here, and why I thought it would be all right to visit and get to know you better."

"What did you have in mind?"

"Oh, I don't know. A few drinks. Maybe a party?"

My stomach gave a lurch as I realized what he had in mind. We had this fish on the line, and the last thing we wanted was to lose him. But there was no way Brady was going to go along in the slightest degree, and much as I loved Betty, I wouldn't be able to even hug the guy. The men in my family, like in most Italian families, hugged all the time, and those in my grandparents' generation even kissed, like with my uncle Pietro. But that was different. Boy, was that ever different. You're the brains, Brady had said. I racked them, and stood back waiting for the cue ball to break the triangle.

"Terry," I said, "you're a very nice looking boy, and a couple of years ago we would have jumped at the chance. But times have changed. Matty and I made a vow that we would not endanger each other's lives with any extracurricular activities."

"I'm negative," Terry almost yelled.

"I'm sure you are," I told him kindly, "but we have passed the stage of checking blood tests. In our wedding ceremony we promised to love only each other, and we intend to stay true to that until God parts us."

Brady was looking at me with what had to be eyes of admiration. Or was it sheer hatred? I wondered what had happened to his stomach when the kid popped the proposal. Unlike some of the guys on the force, neither Brady nor I had ever hassled homosexuals. But that was as far as it went. This thing with Terry had to be kept within those bounds.

"That doesn't mean we can't get together for drinks or maybe do dinner at one of the restaurants," said Brady. "We enjoy having a kindred spirit for company."

He gives me a hard time about using the long words that Carlotta made me learn, and then he goes saying something like *kindred spirit*.

"Oh," said Terry, "we can't really be seen together in public. I don't know what would happen if the others found out. But I would like to know I have a haven here that I can visit and where I can have a few drinks and relax. Or maybe you could just let me watch."

"Would you like another drink, Terry?" I asked.

He checked the Rolex on his wrist. You get to know fancy timepieces when you're dealing a lot with pimps. Watches and foreign cars.

"Oh," he said, "I would have loved that, but I'm due to go on shift. It's been lovely meeting the two of you, and I will take you up on your invitation if only for a place to be myself. I think it's marvelous that you two have made such a vow. I only wish I could find somebody like that."

We walked him to the door, and when Brady pulled it open and saw that nobody was in the hall, he put his arm around my waist and pulled me in to him. I thought Terry was going to get tearful, but he just

THE BROKEN-HEARTED DETECTIVE

blinked a couple of times, waved his hand and was gone. Brady didn't say anything as he walked over to the minibar and pulled out another bottle of beer plus potato chips and peanuts.

"If you get fat on me," I told him, "my eye might start to rove."

16

There were maybe eighty women at the pool when we got there after a late breakfast, and we were the only two men. It was weird walking to our chairs because every cluster we passed went dead silent until we were by them, and then it was like a bird fight had broken out. I caught some of the looks, and there was no doubt that the ladies had made the same assessment as everybody else. Objectively speaking, we were both hunks, even though I had softened up somewhat and Brady's stomach was curving into the male simulation of the fifth month of pregnancy. But all it takes is one whisper, and then it's like the president had signed it into law. Not that there was one woman in that whole bunch who excited your attention, let alone your libido, as Carlotta used to call it when she was ripping open my shirt. It made you understand why it was so easy for funeral directors to look solemn and sorrowful whenever the job called for it. All they had to do was think of the women they were stuck with.

We were getting into the swing of things, however, so we rubbed suntan lotion on each other rather than ourselves, and we kept whispering lurid descriptions of the individual dogs who were sitting around us. I was quite funny, and Brady kept laughing out loud. I asked him softly if he would try giggling instead of sounding like a stallion in pain, but he wasn't able to hold it in control. When I finally lay back on the lounge chair and closed my eyes so that I could concentrate on the pink haze coming through the lids, I thought about Betty cooped up in the desert with all those men around her and how scared she had to be, and things lost their funniness. There are a lot more nice people in the world than there are evil ones, but it is amazing how much trouble just a few of the sons of bitches can cause, whether you're talking about a Saddam Hussein or a Kurt Reich or a kid who pushes drugs on a street corner. That was the thing I missed most about being a cop. Because every time I brought in one of the scumbags, I knew I was saving several good people lots of grief.

Brady could barely swim so he went into the water only to cool off, but I did forty laps in a slow crawl, and it felt so good that when I stopped, I smiled at the woman who was standing next to me. She smiled back and said, "You and your friend seem to be having a good time."

"We don't get away like this very often," I told her. "Mostly it's work, work, work."

"What do you do?" she asked.

What did we do? It took me a moment.

THE BROKEN-HEARTED DETECTIVE

"We have a chain of unisex hair salons," I came up with.

When I sat down next to Brady again, I told him what we did for a living.

"I was thinking more of a flower shop," he said, "or maybe we could have been interior decorators."

We lunched at the pool bar, and then sat in the sun some more until about four o'clock I began to feel light-headed. The doctor had warned me about too much sun, but I was so revved up that I was barely remembering to take my pills. It wouldn't do anybody any good, especially Betty, if I got sick or died so I went back to the room, showered and took a nap in the cool bedroom. Brady had been drinking beer, and chatting with the woman in the chair next to him when I left, and was telling her about doing Madonna's hair for one of her videos. I thought I knew Brady like the back of my hand, but there were sides to him that were beginning to awe me a bit.

We had dinner again at the Flying T, but neither Terry nor any of the hard-looking cases were around this time. Brady had his usual steak dinner, and I ate grilled chicken that was good, but the baked potato had a big brown spot in the middle, and just the sight of it took the edge off my appetite. I was feeling edgy because we hadn't come up with any plan on how we were going to get next to Reich and find out what made him tick. The only possible solution was to cause some uproar that neither the feds nor Reich himself could control or avoid so that in the showdown between them Betty faded out of the picture. The simple thing would be to go to the newspapers and TV stations, but they wouldn't do anything without proof, and all the tracks seemed covered. Something bad could happen to Betty if the thing screwed up, so we had to find an angle that neither side had thought about.

It was almost ten o'clock before we got back to our rooms. Brady was behind me when I unlocked the door, and as I was reaching out to throw the cardboard key on the table, I heard the door slam shut and Brady came barreling into me so hard that both of us went down on the floor. Being knocked down by Brady's body is a little like having a meteor slam into you so it took me a second to turn over and see what the hell had happened.

What had happened was that a guy as big as Brady had been standing behind the door and had shoved him into me after we went by. In addition to his size, he also had a .38 with a silencer screwed on it that was pointing in our general direction. We might have worked something out between us, but a voice saying, "Take it easy and nobody gets hurt," caused us to turn our heads and there were three other guys standing there who had been in either or both of our bedrooms. Their guns were still in their holsters, but it would have been no trouble at all for them to have quickly drawn and had us in their sights.

I recognized two of them from the table Terry had been sitting at the night before, and the first thing that went through my mind was that the kid had played us for suckers. He had been on a reconnaissance mission to check us out, and now we were either dead or disappeared or with faces resembling those of the ladies at the pool. Here we'd been laughing at how we had learned so much from the kid, and all the time we were the ones who were the fools. How far should

THE BROKEN-HEARTED DETECTIVE

we play the innocent parties? It was at least worth a try.

"All the cash we've got is in our wallets," I said, "and our watches aren't worth that much. Take whatever you want, but please don't hurt us."

"We're not going to hurt you, Mary, if you don't scream or do anything else girlie," said the one in the middle of the three. He was the oldest of them all, somewhere between forty and forty-five. Very dark. Almost like he was an Arab of some sort.

"Can we get up?" Brady asked, and I could tell by his voice that he was just this side of losing it. Brady wasn't used to being knocked down, and he had a thing about bad guys. It went against his whole grain, and the fact that the creep was holding a gun on us wouldn't even be weighed on the scale if anger overcame judgment.

"Sure," said the spokesman, and you could tell by his voice that he didn't think a gun was necessary to keep us under control. He assumed we would be too busy wetting our pants to cause any trouble. As I was getting up, I put my hand on Brady's arm and squeezed as hard as I could. He didn't look at me as he slowly moved to his feet.

"Now," said the crew chief, "there's a man wants to talk to you two. He lives down the end of the block next to the mountain, and he's the mountain and you two are Mahomets. So all of us are going to take a pleasant walk there, and nobody will get hurt if nobody makes any trouble. Are there any questions?"

"The police will hear of this," said Brady, and I could tell by his voice that he was back in control.

His remark made the guy laugh, and all the others put smiles on their faces.

"He'll probably talk to you about that too," he said.

"Now Frank and Jim are going to walk ahead of you, and we will be right behind. You don't talk, but if somebody smiles and says 'Good evening' or 'How the fuck are you?' you'll nod and smile back and keep moving. We don't want to hurt you, but we can and will if need be. Is that understood?"

We just looked at him, and a frown went over his face.

"Is that understood?" he yelled, just like the drill sergeant does the first week the rookies are in camp. Sometimes they keep yelling it until the rookies are screaming in return, but we both nodded yes and I added a small grunt, and that seemed to suffice.

It's funny but the thing that bothered me most as we walked to Reich's building was not what might happen to us, but what could happen to Betty if we weren't there to do something about her situation. If there was any doubt in my mind before, this took care of it. I really was in love with that girl.

17

They took us down a service elevator and out a back door to get to their home base. There was one point when I thought Brady might go for the pair in front of us, and I braced to whirl around in a try for the other two, but as we came out the door, they pulled their guns at the same time, and we would have been dead meat. They hadn't searched us so we still had our ankle guns, but there was no chance to go for them unless we could convince them we had to pull up our socks.

There was a guard outside the building we were led to, and he came forward holding an Uzi by his side.

"What's this?" he wanted to know.

"When are you guys going to learn not to ask questions?" said the head man impatiently. "Your job is to guard the perimeter and ask no questions. Period. Even a rookie CIA agent should be able to understand that."

The guard was so mad that I could see his hand tighten on the Uzi, ready to bring it up and maybe spray the area, but he held it in, he just about held it in. Without another word, he stepped back into the darkness, but you could almost see his eyes gleaming.

There were two other guards inside with automatics slung around their shoulders, but they didn't say anything as we walked through and up the stairs. There were carved wooden double doors at the top, and one of the guys in front knocked on the panel. There was no answer for what seemed like a long time, but then a man's voice shouted, "Come!"

And there he was, Kurt Reich, dressed in a red sports shirt and tan slacks, no shoes on his feet. The room was as big as our whole suite with heavy, glass-topped coffee tables scattered around, one of those concert grand pianos, and paintings the size of doors on the walls. It's funny though that no matter how expensive the hotel room there is always the smell that comes from the people who stayed there before you. It isn't just stale tobacco smoke; it's kind of like the air they breathed out of their bodies all mixed together into one.

The two front guards pulled to the side, the two behind us shoved us forward a couple of steps, and there we were face-to-face with the man himself. That close you could see the lines running down his cheeks, and realize that he was near fifty despite his trim waist and well-developed arms. The guy worked out, there was no doubt about that. He looked us over like he was thinking of buying us from a used car lot, running his eyes up and down Brady's body twice.

"So these are Terry's new friends," he said, his voice low and even but the kind that made it to every corner of the room. "Can't say that I blame him."

It took a second for him to relax his mouth into a smile, and as soon as that happened, the four guys laughed out loud. Everybody made damned sure in this group that they didn't laugh until the big man let them know something was funny. There were cops on the force who did the same thing with sergeants, lieutenants and up. I suppose there are people like that everywhere. Like if Hitler or Saddam Hussein laughed, you laughed. If you didn't think it was funny, you died. I wondered if people who didn't laugh when Reich smiled ended up dead. Brady and I didn't laugh.

"I had you brought here," said Reich, "because I want you to be thoroughly familiar with the ground rules that go with friendship with Terry. If either of you have AIDS or have tested HIV positive, my advice would be to go back to your rooms, pack and leave here tonight. If you haven't been tested at all, the same thing applies. But if you have been tested and are negative, it is perfectly all right to continue

THE BROKEN-HEARTED DETECTIVE

the friendship. With my blessing. The boy has been devastated since his friends from Minneapolis left."

I had no idea I had been holding my breath until my chest relaxed and pushed the air out of my nose. He didn't know anything about our relationship to Betty or what was going on. We had been hauled there because he thought we were a couple of gays who were involved with his nephew, and he didn't want his sister's son to get burned while under his jurisdiction. I turned my head a bit and looked at Brady, but he was staring at Reich. How much longer could he hold it? If he blew, our cover went with it.

"You have no right to do this to us," I said, not sure whether my voice was trembling because I was playing a part or because I was maybe scared. "Our work load has been brutal, and we are here to rest and recover our energy. We explained to Terry that we did not wish to be involved, that we could be friendly but that was as far as it could go. Now we want to go back to our rooms and be left alone, or we will complain to the manager."

He thought about this for a minute, his face expressionless but the brain working.

"Let's leave it this way then," he said. "The ground rules I laid down stand, and you can go or stay if you act accordingly. But if you violate the conditions, there will be negative action. And if you complain to the manager or the police, it will go even harder. My arm is long and I can track you down to the ends of the earth if need be. This is just a taste of what could happen if you don't do exactly as I say."

He nodded his head and at that moment I received a crushing blow to the right side of my back that brought me to my knees, fighting to keep from throwing up everything I had eaten for dinner. What I wanted to do was fall to the rug and squirm around, but I was goddamned if the bastards were going to see me do that. I turned my head and looked at Brady, who was still standing, but I could tell that he'd been belted in the kidney too, hard enough to have twisted him up but not enough to knock him to the floor as it had me.

"No," said Reich, and the guy who was standing behind Brady dropped his hand to his side. From the look on his face you could tell he was humiliated that he hadn't been able to bring Brady down the same way the guy behind me had done.

"That was just a taste," he repeated to us. "Now if you are smart, you will forget this incident and carry on your lives. There is no need for you to run away, nor even not to see Terry if you want. You will not be bothered again if you do not break the rules. Rules are very important to me. Good night, gentlemen."

He turned and went through the glass doors to one of the outside patios. The guy who had hit me put his arms under mine and lifted me to my feet. I wobbled a bit but was able to stand. Brady put his arm under mine and turned me around.

"Bring them downstairs," said the underboss, "and see they get on their way."

I stumbled once on the stairs, but we finally made it to the outside patio. Only one guy had gone all the way down with us, and at the bottom he turned and went back up. When we came out on the terrace, the guard was standing there looking at us. He opened his mouth but then didn't say anything. You could tell from his face that he realized they had hurt us up

THE BROKEN-HEARTED DETECTIVE

there, but then he remembered who he was and why he was there, and let it go at that.

We walked slowly all the way back to our place without either of us saying a word. I knew Brady could have gone faster, but he was holding back so that I wouldn't feel more humiliated than I already was. When he had shut the door behind us, he walked over to the minibar, pulled out a can of beer, and drank it down without once taking it from his mouth. Then he sat down on the couch and switched on the television with the remote.

I pulled up my shirt and walked over to stand between him and the TV screen.

"What does it look like?" I asked.

"It's turning blue," he said. "You've had worse."

"What about yours?"

"I've had worse."

"What's going on?" I asked.

He didn't answer.

"Brady, what the hell's with you?"

At first I thought he still wasn't going to answer, but then he turned his head and looked at me.

"You know," he said, "I came along on this deal at the beginning because I thought we had a real case, one that would get our agency started. Then when you told me about your girl, I could understand how you felt, and I wanted to help. But the whole thing's been sort of like when we were on cases involving people we didn't know and who we were never going to see again when it was over. You're my friend, my best friend, but it was basically your problem, and I was just going along to do everything I could to help you. But now it's personal; this guy has made it personal. It's between him and me now. I've been thinking about it. You could decide to call it quits right now and go home, but I couldn't do that. I'd stay right here until I got the son of a bitch. Things are different now, and it bothers me that I didn't feel the same when it was just my best friend's problem. I'd understand if you were pissed off for not getting what you should have from me before this happened. What kind of friend am I?"

"You're the kind of friend that only a few people are lucky enough to have," I said. "You're—"

The knock on the door was gentle, but it was enough for both of us to pull our ankle guns and spread out on different sides.

"Who's there?" I asked, moving to the left as I said it in case they shot where the sound had come from.

"It's the maid, senor," said a woman's voice softly. "I have the clean towels."

"It's late," I told her. "We can wait until tomorrow."

"No, senor," she said. "It must be done tonight."

Brady nodded at me, and I palmed the gun and dropped my hand to the side. Then with my left hand, I turned the knob and pulled the door open to the length of the safety chain. A Mexican girl in the hotel uniform was standing there beside the cart that holds all the stuff for the rooms. She had a bunch of towels over her arm. I closed the door, unhooked the chain, and opened it again just enough for her to slip through. Then I poked my head out and found the hall empty. I closed the door again and rehooked the chain.

The girl went straight to my bathroom and came out with the dirty towels. But instead of going to Brady's bathroom, she stood there looking at us. She was a mousy-looking thing with jet black hair pulled into a knot in back, which seemed to be the style for the maids. Her skin was darker than most, and I wondered if there was black blood as well as Mexican in her. She kept staring. I couldn't figure out what the problem was.

"Yes?" I said.

"What did they do to you?" she asked in a clear voice, straightening her body from the slight slouch it had been in. Brady was there before me.

"Jesus Christ," he said, and it was more religious than surprised. "It's Daphne."

18

It took a few seconds for it to sink in, but even when I realized that Brady had to be right, I still couldn't pick Daphne out of the disguise. One time on a drug buy I was so proud of myself because I had glued on a fake mustache and dressed like a pimp with those black sunglasses and lifts in my shoes and my hat pulled down so nobody could see my hair, and everyone who passed by me in the station, every goddamned one of them, had said "Hi, Vin" without even thinking about it.

She looked darker, plumper and somehow shorter, and her face was just this side of ugly, none of which applied to the Daphne who had knocked Brady on his ass. My father told me once about a movie star who was known as "the man with a thousand faces," and I wondered if Daphne was a relation. Maybe a granddaughter.

"They worked us over a little bit," said Brady, in answer to her question, "but it had to do with his fag nephew. He didn't make us."

"You two have certainly made an impression on everybody in this hotel," she said, dropping the towels on the floor and coming toward us. "Even the maids giggle when you walk by. They had a bouquet of flowers left in one of the rooms, and they were going to put roses on your pillows along with the mints."

Daphne was reporting this in a straight voice. I had the feeling there was not much of a sense of humor in Daphne. Or joy either. I wondered how she was in bed with all that intensity and strength focused on one thing only. A little shiver went through me, and I switched my thoughts to Betty. Sometimes I wonder about myself.

"Daphne," said Brady, "have you taken a job here or is this a hit and run?"

"My name is Juanita Estevez," said Daphne, "and I make eight dollars an hour plus very limited benefits. This is my second day of employment, and I'm thinking of starting a union."

Wrong again. The lady not only had a sense of humor, but she was funny. Or was she being serious? How the hell could you tell?

"Are you thinking of infiltrating Reich's place in that getup?" I asked.

"They shake everybody down before they can come into the building, even the cleaners. It's so thorough that some of the women look forward to it. They'd find the pads and make me in a minute. Russ supervises. Russ supervises everything. I could never get by him."

"Then what is your plan?"

"Probably the only way we can reach him is when he goes to his safe house."

"What safe house? Where does he go?"

"I have concluded that he has a house in the desert somewhere in Arizona or it may even be in Mexico," she said. "They've probably tried to find it, but I'm positive Washington doesn't know where it is. Somewhere not too far from here, I'd wager, but far enough. He never said it, but I'm sure the reason he stays at this place is that the house has to be fairly accessible. It's hard to tell because when he goes to it, he's usually away for two or three days. The trip may take that long, or else he spends some time when he gets there. I used to beg him to take me with him, but the only one who ever goes is Russ."

"Who's Russ?"

She described the guy who had done all the talking when they had come to get us.

"Is he the only one Reich trusts?" I asked.

"As far as he trusts anybody."

"Why does he go there?" asked Brady.

"For one thing, he's got to have millions in cash and gold," she said. "He always comes back with a suitcase of money."

"What about those tapes and transcripts and things that have the government so scared?" I asked her.

"They could be there," she answered.

"You told us he had his blackmail stuff spread out,

and people ready to make them public if something happened to him."

"That could be true, and then again it might not be true," she answered. "The more I think about it the more I feel Kurt would not trust anybody. Maybe he trusts Russ." She stopped to think for a moment. "But I'm not so sure he trusts him that much either."

"What about you?"

"What about me?"

"Did he trust you that much?"

"I got a knife into him, didn't I?" She paused again. "But that was only because I had completely exhausted him."

It popped into my mind again. She exhausted him. Completely. I wondered what it would be like to have that body pitted against yours in bed. How long did it take to notice that a knife was sticking out of your chest?

"But he never took you to his desert house," Brady said.

"One down and one to go." She shrugged.

"Daphne," I said, "do you have some plan for us to follow? The only thing I can think of is to get a sniper's rifle and waste him while he's on the golf course. But Brady and I aren't going to do that. No matter how dangerous he is, no matter how big a threat, we're not going to murder anybody."

"Leave that to me," she said.

"Are you going to get a sniper's rifle and kill him on the golf course?" asked Brady.

"Of course not," she said with a shake of her head. "This is a personal matter. An eye to eye matter. He will know exactly who is doing it."

THE BROKEN-HEARTED DETECTIVE

"Daphne," I said, "this farce has gone on long enough. I want to protect my fiancée from this loony, and I don't want him harassing her anymore, but Brady and I aren't going to help you kill anybody. What we want to do is fix it so the government guys can move in on him. From what you've said they seem to have plenty of evidence against him for prosecution, and if we can just get those tapes and papers away from him, they can do their thing."

"Their thing," said Daphne, "would be to kill him in a minute. You don't really realize what you're dealing with here. It's as though they are their own country within your country, one that makes its own laws about life and death. I'm sure he will die in what will be called an auto accident or something along those lines if they get their hands on him, but it will be an execution no matter what you call it."

"Then why not let them handle it?" I asked. "They'll do your thing for you, and there won't be any blood on your hands."

She held her hands out toward us, turning them over and back three or four times.

"Do you know how much blood is already on these hands?" she asked. "Blood that was spilled because he ordered it? You are not dealing with a human being here. You are dealing with Kurt Reich."

"Do you still love him?" I asked.

That stopped her. Cold. At first I thought it was because it was something she hadn't thought about, but then I realized she wanted to describe it in a way we could understand.

"I still love him," she said simply, "but always in my love there was also hate because of the things he made me do, things I didn't want to do. But most important of all was that I was the only woman in his life. Even when he was away for long periods of time, I could tell when he came back that he had not taken another woman. Not even for an hour. But then it was over. He said that I no longer stimulated him. That was the word he used—*stimulated*. My anger was such that I tried to kill him. But even then I thought he would take me back."

"Hey, wait a minute," said Brady. "You tried to knife him to death, and then you thought he might want you back? You're not making sense."

"That is only because you do not know him as I do. My trying to kill him might possibly have whetted his passion, proved to him how deep my feeling went. At least that's what I dreamed. Until the nurse came along. I knew that was different right away. I don't know what there is about her, but there is something that he needs, that he feels he must have. And when she spurned him, he became obsessed. There was no attempt to deceive me. When I called him, he told me there was now another woman in his life, and I could not come back. He said he would see to it that I would never want for money, and I could always call on him if there was a problem. But I could never see him again. He said he bore me no ill will, that he understood why I had gone to the knife. But if I had done to him what he did to me, he would also want me dead so that no other could ever have me. We may all end up dead while he lives. We shall see. We shall see."

"Jesus Christ," said Brady, "you people make crackheads seem normal."

"Never mind all that," I said. "We know we're

trapped in a loony bin. How is he able to disappear from here with all those government men around?"

"I don't know. One moment he is there, and the next he is gone. One moment he is gone, and the next he is back." You could see her body tremble a bit. "How he leaves and how he returns is beyond my power to find out. When he would be out playing golf, I would search that house from top to bottom, but I never found anything. It is crazy but sometimes I used to think that he is not human, that there is a space ship up there somewhere transporting him to wherever he wants to go."

"Do you think the son of a bitch is off *The Enterprise?*" Brady asked me.

"I think he's just off," I said. "Remember the Gypsy lady we put away for scamming that old lady? This guy may be her nephew. We've just got to watch him until we catch him in a move."

"Why the Christ do you think the feds have those men around him?" asked Brady. "To keep him safe or to try to find out where he goes when he ain't there no more. If this lady who slept with him couldn't figure out how he flies the coop, and the seven dwarfs from the CIA can't solve it, how are two homosexuals from San Bernardino going to do it?"

"Leave that to me," said Daphne.

"Leave what to you?" snapped Brady. "If you couldn't find out where he goes while you were playing house with him, how do you expect to do it when you're making beds or swirling brushes in the toilet bowls? We've got to think of something to flush him out, make him run to his hideaway."

"Why don't we try working it through Terry?" I suggested.

The look on Brady's face was awesome. Whatever the hell was going through his mind made me wonder how well he really knew me. He was waiting to hear more before pronouncing sentence.

"Maybe the kid knows something, and if we get some drinks in him, get him to talk, we may find out what we want," I said hurriedly. "He could know where uncle goes and how he gets there. What the hell else do we have to go on?"

"What we have to go on," said Daphne, "is that we know about them, but they don't yet know about us. I will keep working from my side, and you two do whatever you can from yours. I will admit that what we need is luck to go with everything else, but I have always made my own luck, and I'm sure God will help me when the time is right."

"God," snorted Brady, the Catholic who went to church once a year. "Considering your background, you better ring somebody else's doorbell."

"I will be in touch," said Daphne, obviously not ready to argue theology. She picked up the towels and went out the door without saying another word.

"What did you think of that?" asked Brady.

"I think from now on we better check everyone who comes near us," I said. "The waiter, the golf pro, the desk clerk—any one of them could turn out to be Daphne."

There was a soft knock on the door.

"What the hell did she forget?" asked Brady, moving toward the door. "The roses on our pillows?"

"Don't open it," I hissed, reaching down and pulling out my gun. My words stopped Brady in his tracks. He went to the bureau drawer and retrieved his Be-

THE BROKEN-HEARTED DETECTIVE

retta, then walked over to the door and slid the chain on its hook.

"Yes," he asked, his voice low.

"I'm here from Mr. Frye," a man's voice said.

Motioning Brady to step to the side, I went to the door and opened it as far as the chain would allow. There were two of them out there. I could see the man plainly, but the other one was a little too far to the right. The guy wasn't holding a weapon.

"What do you want?" I asked.

"Mr. Frye sent you this," he said.

"Sent me what?"

He didn't answer, but reached out his hand and pulled the other person into open view. I must have made some kind of sound because Brady ran behind me with his gun ready to shoot. When he looked out, he made some kind of noise too.

For standing there was Betty Wade, holding on to a little black suitcase. I reached up to undo the chain when Brady grabbed my hand.

"Wait," he ordered.

"Miss," he said, "is there anybody else out there with you."

"No," she answered. "Just the two of us."

I slipped off the chain and opened the door all the way.

"Altobelli," said Betty, coming through the door, "I'm home." Both Lucy and Ricky would have been ecstatic to hear the way she stole their line.

19

While Betty and I stood there grinning at each other, Brady dashed into the hall, yelled, "Hey! Hey, wait a minute," and disappeared. I held out my arms to Betty and she came right into them, holding on to me like my three-year-old niece Philomena did when she grabbed one of my legs and wouldn't let go until her father pried her loose with much yelling and swearing.

We were still standing that way when Brady came back into the room, closed the door, bolted it and turned toward us.

"Caught him at the elevator," he said. "Thought he was going to go for the stairs before it arrived, but I got there in time. He wouldn't say anything except that he was 'following orders.' Should have squeezed more out of him, but the elevator came with two fat ladies on it."

"You can't squeeze a man when there are fat ladies present," said Betty, unwinding her hug and stepping back. I could have stayed that way for an indefinite period, but I didn't want to scare her.

"I know I'm here," said Betty, "but I still can't believe it. Did you have something to do with them letting me go, Altobelli?"

I would have given up one of my cases of money if

THE BROKEN-HEARTED DETECTIVE

I could have modestly nodded, but I was always going to be honest with this girl so I shook my head no.

"Then why did they bring me here?" she asked.

"They?" said Brady.

"There were two more waiting down in the car," she said. "I didn't know they were taking me to you so I almost made a break for it when we reached the hotel lobby, but that was when he said we were coming to you so I waited it out. Who are those people and why did they kidnap me?"

"It's a long story, but it all has to do with your friend Reich," I told her.

"Reich? Is he still here?" The look of fear on her face made me smash my right fist into the palm of my left hand so hard that I thought for a second I might have broken something.

"He's at the resort, but you're safe with us."

"What's going on, Altobelli?" she wanted to know. "Why are we here if he's here? Why don't we go? Those men kept grilling me about him. How long had I known him? Had I ever had sexual relations with him? Crazy stuff. What's this all about?"

So I sat her down and told her everything we knew right from the beginning to where we were at that very moment, with Brady adding little bits that I missed. I didn't try to hide anything that might scare her any more than she already was, and at the end I gave her the choice of deciding what we did next—stick it out and get this creep off her back permanently, return to San Bernardino and hope for the best, go someplace to live where nobody knew us.

When I got to there, she interrupted.

"Are you saying that if I want to go to another part of the country, or even the world, where this creep can't find me, you would leave your family and friends and go with me?"

"Sure," I told her.

I had no idea what the problem was when the tears started coming out of her eyes and running down her cheeks.

"It's okay," I told her. "You're safe now. Brady and I are here to take care of you."

"I know that, you damn fool," she snapped. "It's just that everything's been so lousy, and then you showed up and it's better, and now you're willing to give up your whole world just to be with me. You're not being fair, Altobelli. You're not being fair."

"Would you like a beer?" Brady asked her.

"Yes," she said, "I would very much like a beer. And a bath. Did they give you some bubbly stuff to put in the bathtub? And then I want to go to sleep. I want to sleep without waking up every ten minutes. I want to sleep without dreaming."

She took her bath in my room and while she was gone, Brady and I tried to decide what the next move should be. We hadn't made any progress when she came back into the room wearing a hotel bathrobe and a small towel wrapped around her hair.

"The water at that house was all rusty," she said, "and the pressure was so low that only a trickle came out of the shower. They tried to be nice, I guess, but when you never know what's going to happen in the next moment, it's scary. I kept thinking of those hostages in Lebanon."

The anger started to rise in me again, but I wasn't supposed to get my blood pressure up, and my nurse was standing right there so I took some long, slow breaths and let them out easy so nobody would notice.

112

THE BROKEN-HEARTED DETECTIVE

"The cooking was lousy too," she continued. "Do you think I could get a club sandwich?"

Brady suddenly discovered that he was hungry, and I allowed as how I might down a bite or two so we ordered a big spread from room service, and more beer because we had emptied the minibar.

By the time Betty had blown her hair dry and whatever else took a half hour the food had arrived, and we pitched in like it was a party, laughing about this or that, but never talking about what was uppermost in my mind and probably in theirs too. Where did we go from there?

"Okay," I said, when the table was a shambles, "I think I've got a plan."

"What is it?" they both asked at the same time, looked at each other, and started to laugh uncontrollably. There was a little bit of hysteria in that room, and it made my skin feel itchy.

"I think we should get the hell out of here and go back to San Bernardino, and if the son of a bitch tries anything, at least it will be on our turf."

"That makes sense," said Brady, opening the last of the beers.

"Does that mean I'll have to spend the rest of my life looking over my shoulder?" said Betty. "I don't want to do that. I want to get rid of this man permanently no matter what it takes."

A vision of me sighting down on Reich as he stepped up to the second tee went through my mind.

"Then we have to stay and play out the hand," said Brady.

"This guy has a tough track record," I told her. "A lot of things could go wrong, and people could get hurt."

She shivered and drew the bathrobe tighter around her. I wondered about turning off the air-conditioning.

"I don't want anybody to get hurt," she said, "anybody at all. But he told me he'd never quit until I did what he said. I've been having dreams about being alone in a room with him, and he comes closer and closer and closer, and then I wake up all sweaty and with my heart pounding. Maybe it would go away in time, but what if it doesn't? And what if he does what he says he is going to do? What if he gets me?"

"We stay," I decided. "If anybody gets hurt, it's going to be them. And let's not pussyfoot around anymore. We'll sit by the pool and have dinner and go dancing, and if they try something, we've got an excuse to take action. He can't want publicity any more than the government does. He's got a nice setup so why should he spoil it?"

"The guy owes me something personal," said Brady, grinding his fist into the palm of his other hand. "And the guy who hit me. I want to talk to him again."

Betty's eyes were blinking without her realizing it. She was so tired that she could barely keep her head up, but she was so wired that she didn't realize it was happening.

"Okay," I said, standing up, "tomorrow will happen tomorrow. Right now you've got to get some sleep."

"Where am I sleeping?" she asked, standing beside me.

"You can use my bed," I told her, "and I will bunk out here on the couch."

"There is no way I am sleeping alone while Reich is loose on the premises," she said.

A big grin appeared on Brady's face.

THE BROKEN-HEARTED DETECTIVE

"You've got only one choice then," he said, "because the only person in my life that I am afraid of is my wife."

"Can I sleep with you, Altobelli?" she asked. "No sex or anything like that. Just sleep."

"Maybe you'll be able to sleep," I told her, "but it's fine with me."

So there I was lying in bed wearing my briefs and listening to the toilet flush. She came out wearing a long T-shirt that hung just below her hips.

"Do you like this?" she asked, turning like a model. "Those guys bought me some stuff because I didn't have anything with me, and they must have shopped at a discount store."

"Take it off if it bothers you," I told her.

She grinned, switched off the light and popped into bed. Both Brady and I kept our bedroom doors open in case of emergency, and Betty called out, "Good night, Brady."

"Good night, young lovers," he yelled back.

There was a faint light coming through the curtains, and I studied the outline of Betty's head on the pillow.

"Altobelli?" she said.

"Yes?"

"I'd like you to kiss me good night."

I leaned over and carefully put my lips to hers without touching her anywhere else, just soft and easy and nice. Then I fell back against my pillow.

"Altobelli," she said again.

"Yes?"

"That was the sweetest thing that ever happened to me. You're growing on me, Altobelli. You're reaching me beyond gratitude."

115

"Hey," I said, "this is like we've already been married ten years."

Her chuckle turned into a snore. That girl was really tired.

It sounds crazy, but I was almost grateful to that guy Reich.

20

You know how sometimes you understand you're dreaming and you try to wake up, but there's nothing you can do about it so it goes on and on and on. I was lying on the ground but all around me was this fog like you see rising out of swamps in all those horror movies. And in my ear I could hear this soft voice saying, "Don't make any noise. It's me, Vincent, Daphne. It's Daphne. Don't make any noise."

I was trying to pull myself away from the dream and up from sleep when there was a thud by my right ear, and I woke up grabbing my gun from under the pillow and diving for the foot of the bed when Brady's voice came out of the dark.

"Put a light on," he said. "I got him."

There was a thump from the other side of the bed like a body falling to the floor, and Betty yelled, "What's the matter? What's the matter?"

The glow from the clock on the TV set gave me my

THE BROKEN-HEARTED DETECTIVE

bearings, and I reached the wall and flicked on the light switch, turning quickly to fan the room with my gun. Brady was on his knees near my side of the bed, and stretched out beside him, out cold, was one of the maids. Except it wasn't one of the maids. It was Daphne.

Brady made the ID as quickly as I did, and the look on his face was something to behold. Knowing him, I could tell that he felt he had regained some of his machismo by clocking Daphne, but he still couldn't get away from the fact that she was a woman.

"I woke up," he explained, "and something didn't feel right, so I slipped into the living room, and I could see him ... her ... framed against the window light, so I came in here as quick as I could and took him ... her ... out." He was really having trouble with the female part.

"Who is this?" asked Betty, rising to her knees from the floor on the other side of the bed.

"It's Daphne," I told her.

"Who the hell is Daphne?" She was a combination of mad and scared at the same time. Her first real sleep in days and then this happens in the middle of the night.

"Daphne," said Brady, standing up, "Daphne is ... a friend of ours. She's been helping us out in getting you loose."

Betty went tearing around the bed, plopped down beside Daphne and started going over her nurse style.

"Where did you hit her?" she asked Brady.

"I think it was the back of her head," he said.

Betty slipped her hand around the back of Daphne's head, and then looked up at Brady.

"What did you hit her with?" she asked.

"My fist."

"Jesus, Brady, she's got a lump back here the size of a baseball. Get me a cold, wet towel."

"Help me get her on the bed," she told me, and we lifted her up and set her down again.

Brady came back with the towel, and Betty wrapped it around Daphne's head so that it was on the back and on the forehead and also was like a cushion.

"Get me a tray of ice cubes," she said, and Brady dashed out again.

A low moan came out of Daphne, and then her hands shot up and grabbed Betty around the throat. Betty's eyes were beginning to bug out even though I was prying Daphne's fingers loose almost immediately.

"It's all right," I said, pinning her arms to the bed. It took all my strength because they felt like steel pipes. "She's with us," I said. "It's Betty. She's with us."

The arms relaxed and the eyes opened.

"What happened?" she asked.

"Brady thought you were an intruder. He heard you coming through the living room."

"He heard me?"

"That's what he said."

You could tell from the look on her face that she didn't believe that anybody would have heard her when she didn't want to be heard. I hoped it wouldn't spoil her day.

Brady came back with the ice and Betty wrapped it in a towel and made a dent for Daphne to lean her head into.

"I didn't know they had already let her go," said Daphne, turning her head to indicate Betty.

THE BROKEN-HEARTED DETECTIVE

"You knew they were going to?"

"It was being discussed."

"What's going on?"

"They're ready to make some move on Reich. There's talk of pulling the government guards out."

"How do you know all this?"

"I just know." Daphne was not about to reveal her sources of information.

"We've decided to go public with Betty," I told her. "We'll hang around and let the world see her and me being lovey-dovey."

"Lovey-dovey!" said Betty. "Jesus, Altobelli, what kind of woman do you think I am?"

The way I looked at her made her reach out her hand and give my arm a squeeze. She was beginning to get the idea of what kind of woman I thought she was.

"He'll make a move if you do that," said Daphne. "If the government pulls its agents and you go parading around with her, he'll feel it's a challenge. It's his only weakness. He cannot have anyone challenge his authority. He must always be in command."

"Would he pull anything in the open," asked Brady, "or will it be at night like when they waited here for us?"

"With him you must expect the unexpected," said Daphne. "It probably won't be anything stupid that will create a public scene, but you can't even rule that out if it fits into his plan. We can't outfox him; luck will be the only factor we can depend on."

"Hey, Daphne," said Brady, "you lived with the guy for years. Does he put his pants on one leg at a time? Me and Vinnie ain't exactly Iraqi soldiers, you know.

He's the one who had better be worried. And where are you going to fit in on all this?"

"I'll be where I can do the most good," she answered. "But you must remember that he is mine. That is our agreement. Your woman in exchange for Kurt."

"That's our deal," I said. "All we want is to be guaranteed that he will no longer pose a threat to Betty."

"I must go," said Daphne, rising from the bed. "It will be dawn soon and I must not be seen here."

"Shouldn't you rest a while longer?" cautioned the nurse.

Daphne just looked at her.

We walked her out to the living room door.

"Put out the lights," she said, "until five minutes after I have gone."

As Brady was walking over to the light switch, Daphne turned to Betty and said, "You are a foolish woman. You rejected the most thrilling experience any woman could have. I am happy that you did it because I want no one to ever take my place, but you have no idea of how fulfilled your life might have been."

The light went out, the door opened, and she was gone. And we hadn't even thought to ask her why she had come in the first place.

We stood there silently in the dark for I don't know how long until Brady said, "Okay," and switched the light back on.

We all looked at each other without saying anything. I was thinking of what might lie ahead, and it gave me the funny feeling in the middle of my belly. We were dealing with some kind of sickness that had no cure except death.

"Altobelli," said Betty, taking my hand, "let's go back to bed."

She turned to Brady, and said, "This time we're going to close the door. If you hear any noises, don't investigate."

Without saying a word, Brady went into his room and closed the door.

My pillow and sheet were all wet from the ice cubes that had melted through the towel.

"Don't worry about it," said Betty, still holding on to my hand. "We're going to be working my side of the bed."

21

The morning was hot so after breakfast we went over to the resort's shop and bought Betty a bathing suit. The woman produced some bikinis that had Brady gaping in wonder, but despite the disbelief on the clerk's part, Betty insisted she wanted a one-piece suit. When she came out of the dressing room, she looked sexier than any of the girls by the pool who walked around with only their nipples covered and their asses hanging out. Even the saleslady couldn't argue against the bathing suit she probably only trotted out for grandmothers.

When we got to the pool and settled down in lounge

chairs with Betty between us, you could see the funeral ladies were having trouble believing what their own eyes were seeing. Betty slathered oil on both me and Brady, but I was the only one who rubbed it on her. When she was covered all over, and I mean all over, she leaned over and gave me a kiss that made me close my eyes after about ten seconds. When I opened them again, I could see that jaws had dropped in adjoining chairs.

Just before lunch, Terry showed up carrying a tennis racket. The sweat gleamed on his face, and I wondered if a guy with a heart condition like mine could play in that kind of weather without keeling over. When he saw us, he came right over, and his shock was equal to that of all the ladies in the area combined when I introduced Betty as my fiancée.

"But you," he sputtered, looking from me to Brady, "and she," looking from Betty to both of us ... "I'm very glad to see you again," he said, holding out his hand to Betty, which she ignored.

"How is Mr. Reich?" she asked, the sweetness dripping from her voice.

"He's well," he said. "He's ... he's recovered. He'll be happy to know you're here."

"Terry," I said, "give your uncle a message. Tell him if he so much as breathes toward this lady, he'll be able to check his lungs outside his body. Tell him Bill Casey's dead, and all the tapes, videos and memos don't mean rat shit to us, and if he doesn't bug off, we'll be blowing whistles so hard that his ears will ring. You tell him that, Terry. And then I think you should go home to your mother, find a nice boy and settle down."

The redness of his face doubled as he tried to think

THE BROKEN-HEARTED DETECTIVE

of what to say, but he couldn't come up with anything so he turned and left.

"Altobelli," said Betty, putting her hand on my arm, "maybe you were right. Maybe we should just get out of here and go back to San Bernardino. I'll get my old job back and we'll take it from there."

I don't know what I would have said or done, but just then my brother Petey walked over the bridge connecting the big pool with the wading pool, and with him were his wife, Carmen, and their three kids, and ... my heart skipped two beats ... my mother. They were looking around in every direction until my niece Dorita screamed, "There he is. There's Uncle Vinnie."

They practically galloped over to us, my mother bringing up the rear, her little legs pumping away. I jumped to my feet and stood there as they worked their way through the lounge chairs, trying not to believe what I was seeing. What the hell were they doing there? How could I get them away from there?

"Hey, Matt," said Petey, nodding at Brady as they all came up, "how you doing, man?"

We shook hands, and then Carmen gave me a kiss on the cheek, and the three girls looked down at their feet, and my mother threw her arms around my waist, tucking her head into my breastbone.

"Vincenzo," she said. "How's my Vincenzo? How's my baby? You feeling all right? I don't know what I'm doing here. I should be home with Papa but Petey he kidnapped me."

"When Mama told me where you were," said Petey, "I asked the travel agent about it, and she said they were giving terrific package deals. Carmen has been after me to take a few days off so we thought we'd come here and whoop it up with you and Matt."

They were all looking down at Betty while they were talking to us, and she was looking up with a smile on her face.

"Hi, Mrs. Altobelli," she said. "Hi, Mr. Altobelli. You probably don't remember me, but I was Vincent's nurse when he had his heart attack."

They didn't remember her, of course. They were Italian, upset about what had happened to me, and had seen her maybe two times while I was in intensive care, and to them all nurses in white looked alike. My mother and Carmen were appraising her inch by inch, and Petey looked puzzled as he tried to dredge her face out of the past while wondering what the hell she was doing there in the present.

I was still trying to figure out how to handle the situation when a man came over to me and said, "Mr. Altobelli. Mr. Reich would like a word with you."

I looked over at the terrace where his face had pointed, and there he was with three of his people clustered around him. He was studying me and my group with an intensity that made my shoulders stiffen. The pro trying to assess the situation and work it into his plans. I thought for a moment of telling the guy to fuck off, but then I wouldn't have any more information to add to my own assessment and plans.

Before I could make a move, my mother's little face was there pointing up at me.

"Are you all right, Vincenzo?" she asked. "Why do you need your nurse here? Are you having trouble with your ... your ... your you know."

"No, Ma," I said, putting my hands under her arms and moving her back to the side, "I'm fine."

Before she could say another word, I turned and followed the guy to the terrace. Brady and I had tucked our guns into a beach bag, and I assumed he would be pulling it close to him as I left. I wasn't feeling too uneasy because I knew he would be only seconds behind me, and it was doubtful that Reich would pull anything in full view of everybody at the pool. I could feel the blood flowing like it did in the old days when I was still on the force, and Brady and I were about to brace a couple of guys or even a gang on the west side of town. You know what? It felt good. It felt real good.

But when I came to a stop before him and stared into his eyes, then I could feel sweat popping out on me that had nothing to do with the heat or the sun. No wonder he had the government guys acting like he was a hostile government with nuclear capability. When this guy died, the Devil would start hearing footsteps behind him.

22

The eyes shifted to the right of me, and I could feel my shoulders relax a little because it meant Brady was standing somewhere near.

"The warning I gave you two still applies," said Reich, "even though you seem to have shed your plumage."

"Let me give you a little warning," I told him. "My fiancée considers you turtle shit. To her you smell like Gorgonzola, and whenever she thinks back on your touching her, it's all she can do to keep her food down. You talk and act tough when you've got a squad of guys around to cover your ass, but the word is that you're the one who turned your nephew Terry on, and that your real specialty is little boys."

His expression didn't change, but you could tell from the little flicker on his face that nobody had talked like this to him in quite a while. Maybe not ever. I don't know what my reason was for saying what I did, or even if I had a reason, but there was so much boiling inside me that I had to let off some of the steam. He didn't say anything so I kept going.

"Here's what's going to happen," I said. "We know all about your videos and your tapes and your memos and the rest of the crap, but we couldn't care less if it all gets out and the president has to ask for asylum in Iraq. Using you for an example, we've spotted this information with other people in various places, and if you don't leave Betty alone and get off our asses, everybody's going to know about Kurt Reich and his connection to Iran-Contra and drug dealing and the rest of the schmear. It's out of your control now, mister, and if you want to hold on to what you've got, your best bet would be to leave right now for South America and cut your losses."

The two guys standing on his left were Russ and the one who had given Brady his kidney punch. The one on the other side was a stranger. Russ didn't blink an eye while I was doing my spiel, but you could tell that the other two were hearing my news for the first time. They'd look at Reich and then they'd look at me. Russ was the only one who never took his eyes off me.

"You can't deceive me, you ignorant peasant," said Reich. "You know nothing. It's all bluff. You may have had contact with lower echelon people, but the power lies in Washington, and they would never let you spread these lies. You would be in solitary confinement in a federal penitentiary before you could open your mouth all the way. As for your so-called fiancée, I have decided that she is not worthy of being my companion, and you can all go back to wherever you came from without any further attention from me. If you are wise, you will be grateful for my forbearance and run back to your hovels. If you continue to annoy me, you will regret it for the rest of your life."

He was about to turn on his heel when Brady spoke up.

"Wait a minute," he said.

They stopped long enough for him to shove the beach bag into my hands, reach out his long arms, cradle with his long fingers the heads of Russ and the other guy, and smash them together with such force that it sounded like an overripe watermelon dropping from thirty feet in the air. They went down like stones, and I couldn't tell if they were dead or alive. Both Reich and his other guard were frozen to their spots, but I had been with Brady long enough not to be surprised, and I stuck my hand into the beach bag and gripped one of the Berettas.

There was no noise from behind so I looked around and saw that nobody from the pool area had been paying attention to us above them on the tree shaded terrace. Except for Betty and Petey. She had jumped up from the lounge chair, and Petey was already on his way toward us.

"There's more where that came from," said Brady to Reich's retreating back. He had turned and was walking away as if nothing had happened. The third guard stood there for a few seconds, looking down at his buddies and over at Reich, not certain as to what to do, but then he followed the boss without another peek at the two down on the flagstone.

"What the hell's going on?" said Petey as he came up to us.

"Nothing to be concerned about," I said, taking his arm and leading him toward the pool area with Brady coming behind us. "Those guys gave us a hard time in the bar last night, and we were just telling them that we would appreciate it if they didn't do it again."

"Come on," said Petey. "Even Ma wouldn't believe that from you. Are those guys alive or dead?"

"Nothing to worry about," Brady repeated. "A couple of aspirin and they'll be as good as new."

"Jesus," said Petey, "is that what you two did when you were on the force? They don't even do that in Los Angeles anymore."

"Is everything all right?" Betty asked as we came up to the group. The girls were telling Carmen they wanted to get into their bathing suits and swim, and my mother was moving her chair so she could stay out of the sun.

"I think everything is going to be fine from here on in," I told her. "The gentleman says he has lost interest."

It took her a second to grasp my meaning, but then she smiled.

"Really?"

THE BROKEN-HEARTED DETECTIVE

"Really," I told her.

"Vin, can I talk to you a minute?" asked Brady, walking away a bit as Petey watched us, uncertain as to what was going on and what he should do. As the oldest brother, he had always been the most concerned about me, more so than the other four, and he was trying to figure out what the trouble was and what he might do to solve it.

"That fucker's going to go all out now," said Brady, as I came up to him. "Daphne told us true. He won't quit until he's got Betty and we're dead."

"I've got to get my family out of here," I said.

"Yeah, but Petey ain't going to go if he thinks you're in trouble."

"Shall I fill him in so he at least will send Carmen, the kids and my mother home?"

"We've got to do something because here he comes now."

"What the hell's going on?" asked Petey as he came up to us.

"I'm going to give it to you the short way," I told him, "and later on we can fill in the details. Betty is the woman I want to marry, and that creep's been hounding her real bad. He's a dangerous man, but Brady and I can handle him. What you've got to do is take the family home so we can straighten it out without them being caught in the middle."

"I'm not going to leave if you're in trouble."

"Petey," I said, "your wife, your kids, Mama. We can't have them around. We've got to think up an excuse for you to take them back right away."

"They'll suspect something. We'll stay the night and then I'll tell them the hotel reneged on the special and we have to go someplace else. I'll drive them home and then I'll come back here."

"Whatever," I said. "But they can't stay here."

"Okay," he agreed. "We'll all have dinner and hang around, and in the morning I'll take them out of here."

"That will work just fine," said Brady.

Even as he was saying it, I had the funny feeling in the middle of my belly. God might have been busy somewhere else and didn't hear what Brady said.

23

A guy showed me a picture once that was supposedly taken in Hiroshima just as our atomic bomb exploded. There's a man in the front of the picture walking toward you and a dinky car coming the same way, and in the background you can see the mushroom cloud starting its climb. But the shock wave hasn't arrived where the guy and the jalopy are situated so they have no idea that in a couple of seconds they are going to be nuked into eternity.

Carmen and the kids and my mother didn't have a clue about what was happening between us and Reich, and although Petey sensed something about the situation, he couldn't comprehend, like any other normal person, what we were dealing with in the case of a geek who had to be at least crazy and at most craziest. The only person in the world who scared Brady was his wife, and although he was well aware of how dangerous Reich could be, he had never come across anybody or anything he couldn't handle. Betty was spooked, there was no doubt about that, even though she tried to keep up a brave front for my and everybody else's benefit. As for me, the only thing I really worried about was how much my heart could take when push came to shove. The doctor had told me to live a normal life, but to avoid "physical strain and nervous tension." Yeah.

We spent the rest of the afternoon at the pool with the kids getting out of the water only for sodas and the rest of us lounging on the chairs and watching my mother and sister-in-law try to pump Betty about who she was and where the hell she fit into my life. She handled it with the calmness of an intensive care nurse even though they never relented for a second. At one point Brady stood and wandered up to the terrace where we had left the two Reich guards somnambulating, as my captain used to describe it whenever guys in a patrol car were caught knocking off forty winks on a slow night.

"Gone," he said softly as he drifted by me on the way back.

Had they crawled or been carted off while we were looking the other way? It was amazing that nobody had stumbled across them and made a big deal about it. But the funeral ladies were leaving the next day, and they were too busy making plans for the fall convention in Dallas to notice anything but each other. It could have been that their husbands saw the bodies lying on the terrace and had removed them "discreetly" from force of habit.

Finally, the girls squirmed out of the pool and said they were hungry so we decided to go back to the rooms, clean up and then have dinner together at the Flying T. The main thing that worried me was what my mother was going to say if she saw the size of the prices on the menu. She didn't read words too well, but she was hell on numbers with dollar signs in front of them. As for Reich, I shut him out of my mind. It was possible he would pull out rather than have us blow the whistle on him. And if he didn't, we'd handle whatever happened next. I guess I was feeling a little smug about the way Brady had cracked their heads together like coconuts. Goddamn but he was strong.

Betty said she had nothing to wear so I took her to the shop on the way back to the room, and after I promised that she could pay me back, she bought a dress off the rack that fit perfectly and made her look so beautiful that I choked up a little looking at her. The night before had been even better than the first time, and I knew that with her it would get better each time no matter how many years we lived together. I wondered about that even as I thought it over. The last thing I wanted to do was push her too hard before she was ready. Tough as it was for me to swallow, I had to admit to myself that she had not been thinking about me the way I had been concentrating on her while we were apart. Right then she was grateful and appreciative and maybe even felt she owed me something for riding in from the west to save her. Maybe she was even beginning to feel a little something stirring inside her. Whatever happened, it wasn't going to be easy. When my mother asked her if she was

Catholic, she didn't try to hedge at all. She said she was not only not Catholic, but she didn't believe in any organized religion. My mother turned and gave me a look that made me shiver in the blistering heat.

When we reached the dining room, we not only found the family already there, but they had a huge plate of nachos piled in the middle, which the kids were cramming down their throats as fast as their hands could move.

"They couldn't wait," Petey explained as we sat down, "so I figured I'd get some food into them before they drove us nuts."

The kids wanted hamburgers and fries, and Petey, Brady, my mother, Carmen and Betty ordered mesquite grilled sirloins. I had the broiled mako shark.

"I know I shouldn't be eating red meat," Betty said to me, "but for some reason I kept thinking about steak while I was with the government men. I'll give you a bite of mine if you want."

"No, thanks," I told her. "My nurse is very strict about my diet."

She smiled and reached over to give my hand a squeeze. Without thinking, I turned to see if my mother had caught it, and sure enough her eyes were focused like a laser on our intertwined fingers. I tried staring her down, but she wouldn't look up from the hands, so I said the hell with it, pulled my fingers from Betty's and then put my arm lightly around her shoulders. I was thirty-two goddamned years old, and even though my mother and brothers still thought of me as the baby of the family, I was entitled to a life of my own.

As I looked at Betty's profile while she was talking across the table to Carmen, Reich's face burned into my brain, and I could feel the rage shooting from my toes to the top of my head. In that separate building not too far from where we were sitting was one man who was making all our lives miserable. If he weren't there, if he disappeared from the earth—I stopped there. What had happened at Tony Pardo's wasn't that far behind me, and I still thought about the two men who had disappeared from the earth at my hands. Reich killed. Pardo killed. Vinnie Altobelli wasn't a killer. I jumped as my brother Petey slapped me on the shoulder.

"Can I see you for a minute?" he asked.

We walked over to the bar area where waiters and waitresses dressed as cowpokes were trying to help the funeral people toast their final night of revelry before they returned to hometown decorum and Kiwanis meetings.

"Fill me in on everything," he said.

I hesitated for a minute, worried that my big brother would feel it his duty to handle the whole thing by himself, but then I told him the situation in the form of a police report.

"I can't believe the government is mixed up in something like this," said Petey.

"Believe it," I told him. "The last president in this country who didn't let politics come first was George Washington."

"What are you going to do?"

"I don't know. I'm coming to the conclusion that we should just go back to San Bernardino and play it by ear. The problem is that Betty spent two weeks taking care of him, and a nurse gets to know her patients inside out, and she's afraid that he will never give up until he gets her. I've had two sessions with him, and I'm convinced that he's crazy like Hitler and Saddam were crazy. Once they get their minds set on something they don't quit no matter how many lives are wasted. The guy has been having his way for so long that he can't bear to have anybody go against him. It's like he is an American dictator with both the government and the cops on his side. I don't think either bunch likes it, but they follow orders."

"If you were still a cop, would you follow orders like that?"

It was almost like he had hit me in the head with something real hard. What would I have done if I had known that something was wrong, and I had been ordered to leave it alone? What would Brady have done? Would I have tried to do something about it anyway? Would I have quit? This was something Brady and I would have to discuss. Even if it couldn't apply to the past, it might come up in the future, and I wanted it to be straight in my mind if it ever happened.

"I don't know," I told my brother Petey. "I think I might have, but now I know it's wrong."

"I think you should leave with us in the morning," he said.

"I'll talk it over with Brady and Betty, and we'll see."

Everyone but me had dessert. I almost did but I wanted to impress Betty with how well I was sticking with my diet and taking care of myself. She wouldn't want to hook up with a guy who was going to fall apart on her in a few years.

When we returned to the lobby, Petey said they'd get the kids and Ma tucked in and then come over for another beer. I knew he was going to work on me some more about leaving with them in the morning, but what could I say? They were there in about a half hour, but I never let Petey get where he could talk to me alone. He didn't want Carmen to know anything was wrong so he couldn't push it too hard, and after we finished all the beer in the minibar, and chatting about this and that, they went back to their suite. He hadn't yet told Carmen they were leaving, and she was all full of plans for the next day.

Because we had eaten so early, it was only ten o'clock, but I kept thinking about getting in bed with Betty again, and was wondering how I could suggest it without pushing it too far. Take it easy, I kept telling myself. Don't spook her. So we were sitting watching a rerun of "LA Law," with me figuring that eleven would be okay to suggest going to bed when there was a knock on the door.

Brady and I were pulling our guns out as we headed toward it when I heard my brother Petey calling, "Vinnie. Vinnie."

I unchained the door and yanked it open. Petey was standing there with a wild look on his face, and I could feel the cold rushing into my stomach.

"It's Ma," he said. "We can't find her. Ma's missing."

24

Brady took charge. I made a shot at following what I had learned about things like this in eleven years as a cop, but my mind was jumbled at thoughts of my mother being lost somewhere or hurt or even dead, and I couldn't handle it right. So Brady organized our family searching party, and when that didn't work, he notified the night manager, and they put together a crew of bellboys and maintenance people, but nothing came of any of it.

Mama was staying in one of the bedrooms with Theresa, the youngest one, but the kid had fallen asleep before her grandma had gone to bed, and didn't know what had happened. The other two didn't hear anything either because they were watching television in Petey and Carmen's bedroom with the door closed.

Mama's nightgown was still in her suitcase because she never unpacked when she had to go somewhere for a couple of days or even to Italy. That way she was ready to return home at a moment's notice. When Petey and Carmen had left her to visit with us, she was eating a bag of peanuts and drinking a can of prune juice from the minibar because she thought they were free.

At midnight we called in the local cops, and a squad car was there in a half hour. They asked all the right questions, made the usual notes and said they would arrange for people to start searching as soon as it got light.

"There are a lot of canyons around here that she could have wandered into," the sergeant said. "It could take some time."

"She wouldn't have wandered anywhere," I told him. "She wouldn't have left the rooms. She's scared stiff when she's anywhere but her home territory. Somebody did something to her."

"We have had a few burglaries here," said the sergeant, "but never any violence. You people aren't rich like the guy staying at the big house. Why would anybody want to kidnap her? Hey! Where are you going?"

I didn't even turn around to tell him anything, but headed right across the grounds to the presidential suite. "That son of a bitch," I heard myself saying. "That filthy son of a bitch."

I was almost all the way up the steps before two guys came at me and grabbed my arms when I tried to shove them out of the way.

"Hey," said one. "Where the hell do you think you're going?"

"Reich has got my mother in there," I told him, "and I'm here to get her. Let me go."

"Wait a minute. Wait a minute. Nobody's mother is in there. It's just Mr. Reich and his regular staff."

"My mother's missing," I yelled, "and he's got to have her in there."

"Stop it," ordered the guard, putting a soft choke hold on me. "We've been here right along, and nobody has gone in or out who didn't belong here. Your

THE BROKEN-HEARTED DETECTIVE

mother's the lady who's missing I take it. We heard about it. But there's no way she can be in there. No way."

I stopped shoving, stepped back and looked at them.

"Nobody's perfect," I said. "They could have slipped her by you."

"Hey," he said, "I'm sorry about your mother, and I hope you find her soon, but there is absolutely, positively no way she could be in this house."

"Let me just look," I asked him. "What harm could it do if I just look? You go with me. All of you go with me. But just let me check it out."

"Sorry. We can't let you do that. Our orders are to keep out everyone but the people Mr. Reich says can come in. You'd have to get the okay from him."

"Then go ask him," I pleaded. "Just ask him."

The two guards looked at each other, and then one said to the other, "You keep him here. I'll be right back."

While he was gone, the guard and I didn't say anything to each other, just stood there waiting. In five minutes the guy was back.

"Mr. Reich said your mother isn't in the building. He asked his regular guys and they said they hadn't seen anyone. He asked me to tell you that he was sorry that your mother was missing, and that he hoped she would be found soon."

"Was he laughing?"

"What?"

"We've got a thing going with the son of a bitch because he's harassing my girl, and I know he's done something with my mother."

"You're the guy," said the guard. "You're the one

who was here the other night with the big fellow. We heard about that. You're the nurse's boyfriend? We heard she was here. Jesus. The prick can sure hassle people, can't he?"

"Shut up, Tom," said the other guard. "Look, mister. We're sorry about your mother, and we hope everything turns out all right, but there's no way she can be in this building, and there's no way we can let you through. Now why don't you go back and look for her where she might be?"

I stood there for a minute, a whole minute, but they didn't say anything more, just looked at me with those stone faces that pros put on when they've laid down the law to somebody. Christ, I'd done it myself. So I turned and went back to the lobby where they had set up headquarters for the search parties. Both Petey and Brady were there.

"I called home," said Petey, "and the boys are driving out. They should be here in about four hours because Brady called some cop, and they're getting an escort to the border. They're organizing some volunteer groups in town, and maybe we can get some help from the National Guard."

"Where've you been?" asked Brady, as my brother went off to confer with some guy in a green Ranger uniform.

"I went over to Reich's house."

"I've been thinking about that. What happened?"

"Two guards stopped me, and when I told them I wanted to check out the house, they said there was no way my mother could be in there, that they kept up a twenty-four-hour perimeter, and no one had seen her."

"They could have been lying."

THE BROKEN-HEARTED DETECTIVE

"I don't think so. These were the government guys. I asked them if I could search the house, and one of them asked Reich, and he said my mother wasn't there but he was sorry she was missing."

Brady cocked his eyebrows.

"What do you think?" he asked.

"It's got to be him. Nothing else figures out right. Maybe he hasn't got her in the house, but she could be stashed anywhere. Matt, I'm going to kill that son of a bitch. If he's done anything to my mother, I'm going to take him out."

"Slow down. Don't lose your cool. We're going to find her. She's tough, that lady, and she's going to make it."

A chill went through me as I heard the echo of Brady saying that to how many people over the last eleven years. I'd said it myself in the same tone of voice, most of the time knowing that it was just whistling in the wind.

I spent the next few hours pacing, fruitlessly trying to come up with a halfway decent plan. It was after dawn when a bellman came over to me and said I had a call.

It was Reich. From the first sound of his voice I knew who it was, and I shivered, probably from the sweat and the chilled air. Or maybe it was from him. Did the man scare me?

"Have you found your mother yet?" he asked.

"No." I wasn't going to play any games.

"Perhaps if you and Miss Wade would drop in on me, I might be of some help in locating your mother."

"Listen, creep," I told him. "I know you're mixed up in this, and if I could get through the goons around you, I'd be pulling your guts up through your throat.

You're going to lose a finger for every one of her hairs that's mussed. I'm not bringing Betty over there. Under any conditions. Then you'd have two of them instead of one. But I'm coming over there again right now, and this time I'm coming in. Do you get it?"

He chuckled. The son of a bitch chuckled.

"No guns," he said, "and nobody else, especially your large friend. This will be between us. As a matter of fact, don't tell anybody that you are coming here. If you do not follow instructions, who knows what might happen to you or even someone you love." And he hung up.

I didn't even think twice about it. Without saying a word to Matt or my brother, I went back to the room and put my guns in the bureau drawer. What I was doing was stupid, I knew, but I also knew that my ma was missing, and we were getting nowhere. However, I put a note in with the guns telling what I was doing. If something happened to me, eventually someone would come across it, and they could take it from there.

The guards let me right through this time, and another one on the inside led me up the same steps as before. Reich was standing in the middle of the room with four of his guys scattered around. Terry wasn't with them.

"Well," said Reich, walking toward me, "the young man has come to look for his mama."

And he backhanded me across the face so hard that I was knocked to the side maybe four steps. As soon as I caught my balance, I went for him, but hands grabbed me and held me tight despite my lunging.

"Now," said Reich, "we can get down to some serious business. You have frustrated and annoyed me long enough. After we have some fun teaching you a bit of discipline, you'll be able to join your mother and live in peace forever after. The first thing you will do is kiss my shoe. From my experience with you, I know you will fight it, but it will be in vain. Eventually you will kiss my shoe. You can make it as easy or difficult as you want. And within the day I will have the recalcitrant Betty in here. She will kiss something too, but it will be more pleasant than my shoe. This is a little incentive to get you going."

Just as he was pulling back his right fist, the door opened and seven men spilled into the room, spreading out to all the corners. Two of them were the guys who had braced us the first afternoon we scouted the house, and I also recognized the one who had been on guard when we were brought there the first time.

"Mr. Reich," that agent said, "we've been reassigned and we're leaving."

25

That must have been something to walk into, me down on my knees with guys holding each of my arms straight out so that if I even breathed too hard, they could break my shoulders with one little twist. But as far as reaction from the federal guys went, we could all have been sitting there drinking tea with our pinky fingers stuck out. These definitely were not the seven dwarfs; they were big and all their expressions were exactly the same.

Reich brought his fist back to his side and squared himself off like it was a formal inspection.

"What is the meaning of this?" he demanded. "I have heard nothing from Washington. You men have been assigned to guard my perimeter and carry out my assignments. You have no authority to leave, and I will not permit it."

I couldn't see the guy's face because they hadn't eased up on the shoulder holds, but I could tell from his voice that this was one of the more satisfying moments of his life.

"Mr. Reich," he said, "you have nothing to do with it. We were here because we were ordered to be here by our superior, and now he has told us to leave."

"But when will the replacements arrive, Stevens?" asked Reich. "You can't leave until they are in place."

"I don't know when they will get here or whether any are coming here. My orders concern only our leaving. Immediately."

"Leave then," yelled Reich. "Get the hell out of here. But I'm about to call Washington, and when I do, both you and your so-called superiors will be in grave trouble. I promise you, Stevens, you'll regret this."

"He's coming with us," said Stevens.

"What?"

"We're taking that man with us."

"Who?"

"The man on the floor. We're taking him out of here with us. You two let go of him."

THE BROKEN-HEARTED DETECTIVE

Like one, the faces of the guys holding me turned to Reich. He wasn't paying any attention to them.

"How dare you say anything like that," he said. "This is none of your business. You get out of here and leave me to mine."

"He's coming with us," said Stevens, his voice as even as if he were reciting somebody his rights. "It is apparent what will happen to him if we leave him here, and we cannot be a party to that. Now let him go."

Either his voice or his manner was enough to make an impression because the fingers pulled away from my arms, and since they had squeezed the strength out of them, they dropped to where my knuckles hit the floor. I couldn't use my hands to push myself up so I stayed on my knees trying to shake some strength back to the fingers. I finally managed to stand.

Reich was there stiff as stone, his lips pulled together so tight that you could see dimples in his cheeks. He raised his right hand in the air as though he were going to say something, but then dropped it again. I looked around the room, and the agents were spread out in a nice pattern, their hands ready to draw their weapons if needed. Reich's four guys looked confused.

"Let's go, mister," said Stevens, putting his arm out toward me like you do when you're politely telling somebody to go ahead of you through a door.

"Mr. Stevens," I said.

"Yes."

"My name is Vincent Altobelli," I told him like I was applying for a job, "and I was a policeman for eleven years before being disabled. My fiancée is a girl named Betty ..."

"We know all about Miss Wade," said Stevens.

"This guy here"—I turned to point my finger at Reich—"has been threatening—"

"We're aware of the situation, Mr. Altobelli."

"My mother is missing, and—"

"We know about your mother, Mr. Altobelli."

"He's got to be the one responsible for her being missing," I said, pointing my finger again at Reich, "and I have a feeling she's being held somewhere in this house."

"We're positive no one like your mother was brought in here past us, Mr. Altobelli."

"Please," I said. "Please. Would you just help me search the house in case they slipped her by you some way? It's my mother. If she's not here, then I can concentrate on looking somewhere else. But she's got to be here. Or I've got to be sure that she isn't. You can take me out of here now, but I'm going to be coming back. You people are trained in this sort of thing. It's my mother."

"Is it all right with you, Mr. Reich, if we give this gentleman a hand?" asked Stevens, and I couldn't tell if he was being serious or sarcastic.

Reich raised both hands in the air the way you do when somebody suggests something ridiculous.

"You have already ruined your career," he said. "You might as well make complete fools of yourselves."

So we went through that house for nearly two hours while Reich and his men stayed in the big living room. The agents were very serious and very thorough, banging on walls and removing clothes from closets, but we didn't find a thing. Stevens finally came over to

THE BROKEN-HEARTED DETECTIVE

me and said that there was nothing more they could do without special equipment.

"They couldn't have gotten her into this house without our knowing it, Mr. Altobelli," he said. "I'm sorry we couldn't find her here, but she has to be somewhere else."

We didn't see Reich again because we were on the ground floor so the eight of us just went out the door.

"Why were you pulled off the job?" I asked Stevens as we walked toward the main building. "Has something changed?"

"I'm not at liberty to discuss my orders, Mr. Altobelli," he said.

"I appreciate your taking me out of there," I said. "It was stupid of me to go there in the first place, but I'm so worried about my mother that I had to take the shot. I don't know if I would have ended up dead, but it's probable that I might have wished I was."

"Reich is an aberration," said Stevens. "We don't have people like that anymore. Don't judge us by his actions."

His voice had sounded a little strained when he said that, and I wondered what it had been like for him and his men to act as guards for scum like that.

"Here's where we turn off," said Stevens, when we came near the parking lot. "I hope you find your mother soon. My mother died when I was four years old, but I can picture her right now exactly as she was."

He held out his hand and we shook. It's strange, isn't it? Here he'd been my enemy because he worked with my enemy, and just then when he left, I felt like a friend was going away. He'd saved my life. I was sure of that, and never again would I lose my cool enough to fall right into Reich's hands. I should have brought Brady and the reporters who were wandering around doing a story on the missing lady along with me, and even Reich wouldn't have dared to pull anything with that crew waiting outside. Maybe we could convince some of the reporters to check into Reich while they were there to do the thing on us. No. If he had her and she was still alive, it might be enough to put her over the edge.

As I walked into the lobby, Betty came toward me with one of Petey's kids. Except that it wasn't. When they were close enough, I saw that it was Bridget, Bridget Burns.

"Where've you been?" asked Betty, taking my arm and squeezing a bit. "Nobody knew where you were."

"I was checking out a lead," I said, "but nothing came of it. Anything new here?"

She shook her head and I could see tears forming in her eyes.

"Bridget saw it on the TV news this morning," she said, "and came out to see what she might do to help."

I looked down at the tiny woman. My mother would look big next to her.

"The government guys helped me look through Reich's house," I said, "because I was sure he had to be mixed up in this. We tossed the whole place, but we couldn't find a thing. There's no place he could hide her."

"Maybe he's got her in President Ford's tunnel," said Bridget.

26

"What are you talking about, Bridget?" asked Betty.

"There's a tunnel on the ground floor that leads into a cave that goes somewhere outside the property," said Bridget.

"How do you know about it, and why is it called the President Ford Tunnel?" I asked, not certain of what she might be talking about.

"In 1978, Ford came here to be in a golf tournament, and he had his wife with him, and she came down with some kind of virus. So the hospital sent me out to take care of her, and I lived in that house for four days."

"But what's that got to do with a tunnel?" I asked.

"The president would be out playing golf all the time or speaking at dinners somewhere, and whenever Mrs. Ford was asleep, which was most of the time, I would wander around the house. There were some Secret Service agents who were still guarding him even though he wasn't president anymore, and one of them took a shine to me. He called me 'Grumpy,' but there wasn't any meanness in it, and he would tell me about famous people he had guarded, and we got along fine. One day he took me down to the bottom floor and said there was an escape tunnel

149

there in case someone tried to kill the president, and he dared me to find it. I got tired of the game after a while, and he said he'd show me. Can you guess where it was?"

We just looked at her.

"There's a giant fireplace that's set on the side where the wall butts the mountain. You could roast a palomino in there. He reached in to the right-hand side, pulled a lever, and a whole metal section folded back. He only let me peek in, but there was one light bulb lit, and I could see it was like a big room carved out of rock. He said it hooked into an old mine shaft and ended up in one of the canyons."

"How did he find out about it?" asked Betty.

"He said he was in the advance party and he got to talking to one of the old caretakers who told him about it, but that the hotel people never mentioned it when they moved in. The way hotels have turnovers in people all the time it could be that the old fellow was the only one who remembered it."

I stood there thinking about what Daphne had told us, how Reich would suddenly disappear and then would be there again, and she never figured out how he did it. I had glanced at the fireplace when we had been searching that big room, but it looked as solid as the mountain behind it, and Stevens's men had gone by it the same way. Brady came through the front door and walked toward us.

"I just talked to Sergeant Renzi," he said, "and both the Tucson and the state police are calling off the search unless there's some kind of development."

"We've got something," I told him, my voice breaking a little because in my gut I felt that this was where they were hiding Mama. Dead or alive.

THE BROKEN-HEARTED DETECTIVE

I didn't want that to go through my head, but it was something that had to be faced. Dead or alive? "Bridget says there's a tunnel that goes from the fireplace on the bottom floor of Reich's place. He could be holding her in there. Let's get the cops and go look."

Without saying a word, Brady whirled around and headed out the door again, returning in three minutes with Renzi, the police sergeant who had been decent to us when we were having trouble with the hospital people. I quickly told him what I had learned.

"We can't go in there," he said.

"Why not? It's hotel property, not his house. Hell, call in for a search warrant."

"The feds told us the place was off limits," said the sergeant. "It's under federal jurisdiction, and we can't touch it."

"But the federal people are gone," I said. "They just pulled out. They're not guarding it anymore."

"They didn't say anything to us. I'll call in. Maybe they talked to the chief, but until I get the okay from headquarters, there's nothing we can do."

"My mother's in there, man," I yelled at him. "You just can't walk away."

"Hell," he said, "if it was just me, I'd go in with you alone even without a search warrant. But I can't do it. Let me call in and ask, and I'll get right back to you."

Brady's eyes locked onto mine, and we stared at each other, our minds working on the same wave length.

"Do you want to wait to see what he says, or do we just go now?" he asked.

"Go where?" asked Betty before I could nod my head. "That man's got seven killers in there with him, and it would be stupid for just the two of you to try anything. This is no time for macho heroics. If it wasn't for me, none of this would have happened, and it's hard enough for me to bear that your mother's missing without you two being killed. The policeman said he would be right back. You've got to wait those few minutes because if something happened to either one of you, I would never be able to forgive myself." Her eyes were full of tears as she moved in two steps and put her arms around me.

"Please, Altobelli," she said, "just a few minutes."

Before I could answer her, Renzi returned with another cop beside him, both carrying shotguns.

"The chief wasn't there," he said, "but the lieutenant said he knew of no change of orders, and as far as he was concerned, the place was still off limits."

We were all staring at the shotguns, and he noticed where our eyes were pointed.

"What the hell," he said. "The lieutenant didn't say he knew that the orders weren't changed. He admitted they could have been changed, but he said we would have to get an okay from the chief when he got back from Yuma. What the hell! Let's go see what's in that house."

Despite our ordering them to stay behind, Betty and Bridget insisted on following us. We didn't have time to argue. They promised they would stay out of range. My brother Petey wasn't around, but I didn't want to take the time to find him so we all trailed after the two Tucson policemen while the guests we encountered stared at us like they couldn't believe what they were seeing.

THE BROKEN-HEARTED DETECTIVE

The sergeant stopped us just before we turned the corner where the house would come into view.

"Okay," he said, "you guys are pros so I don't have to tell you what to do. What I'm going to do is go right up to the front door, knock and identify myself. You people cover me, and be ready to do whatever the hell has to be done. Al."

The patrolman named Al moved up the steps with the sergeant, and Matt and I stuck ourselves behind columns on either side. I turned around to look but couldn't see either Betty or Bridget so I figured they were keeping their word about staying out of the way. Standing to the side of the door, the sergeant knocked, and cocked his head to the side to listen for a reply. Nothing. He knocked again. Nothing. Then he rapped the door with the butt of his shotgun, and from inside we could hear a woman's voice call, "Just a minute."

My heart jumped as I tried to make it be my mother's voice, but it wasn't. I knew it wasn't. The policemen stood to the side of the door and watched as it came ajar. Then it opened all the way, and this nifty looking blonde stepped out. She was dressed in one of those Desert Storm jumpsuits that were all the rage for a while after the war, and she was holding a Beretta in one hand and a Glock in the other, a two-gun woman. The cops shifted their shotguns so they were pointing right at her belly, but she seemed to take no notice.

"They're gone," she hollered, and you could tell that she was making sure that Matt and I could hear her. The shotgun muzzles were practically tickling her, but she was directing her message to us.

"Hand over the guns," the sergeant yelled at her,

153

the adrenaline pumping his voice up about two octaves. You could tell that his finger was putting a little pressure on the trigger.

"Don't shoot," Matt shouted, zooming from behind the post and running toward the stairs. "Don't shoot. It's Daphne."

27

I wondered what kind of a costume Daphne came up with for Halloween because she sure could change herself into anything she wanted. The blond wig and heavy makeup exactly matched that of most of the bimbos from New York who were staying at the resort, and I would have walked right by her if I had met her on one of the paths. Even if I had checked her out because she looked damn trim in that jumpsuit, I wouldn't have made her as Daphne. Either I was slipping or Brady was getting better in his old age.

The cops were still uncertain of what to do about the guns in Daphne's hands, but when she dropped them to her side, they eased off with the shotguns. She was already explaining things to Matt by the time I reached them, and I caught something about the cleaning crew finding nobody to let them in when they arrived at the regular time.

"So I came over to take a look," said Daphne, "and

nothing was stirring. The doors were all locked, but I got in through the back one, but there was nobody here. Some of their stuff is still in their rooms, and they left a couple of guns besides these, but all eight of them are gone, and there's nothing to indicate where or when."

"The fed—" I began to tell her, but she interrupted.

"Yes, yes, I know," she said impatiently. "The agency men are gone. Frye's got to have something new cooking. They wouldn't have done this if ..." She looked at the two policemen and stopped talking. This was family business and she didn't want any outsiders knowing more than they had to.

"Do you have any idea when they might have pulled out?" asked Brady.

"No!" she exploded. "They've disappeared just the way Kurt and Frank would when I lived here. There's no way ..."

"There is a way," I said. "There's a hidden tunnel through the fireplace downstairs."

She whirled and was gone through the door before I could say anything more. Brady zipped after her, but before I could move my arm was grabbed from behind, and there were Betty and Bridget with their mouths starting to open with questions.

"They're gone," I said, "but we're going to check out the tunnel."

I looked at the two cops who had made no move to go through the door.

"This is as far as we can go without orders from on top," said Renzi. "The lieutenant would fry us if he found out what we already did. I'm sorry. We'll report it when we get back to the station so you may be hearing from us again. I hope you find your mother."

Once again I heard the tone in a cop's voice when he's telling somebody that things are going to be all right when he's pretty damned certain that they aren't. Even though I knew he meant well and that I had done the same thing myself dozens of times, a flash of hatred burned through me. How many people had felt that burst when I had ladled out the same words? I tried to smile at him as I went through the door, but I couldn't quite make it.

"Listen," I said to Betty and Bridget as we made our way to the stairs, "there's the chance that there's still somebody hanging around in here, or that these people can come back. So you stick behind me and be ready to jump ship if a mouse squeaks."

Just then there came a hell of a bang from metal hitting metal at the bottom of the stairs, and I went tearing down there. Brady and Daphne were standing in front of the fireplace, and he was about to give the right side of it another whack with a metal chair he was holding in his hands. When he swung around to get extra force into his attack, he saw me and stopped.

"There's no way there can be some kind of a gate there," he said, breathing a little heavy. "There's no hook or catch or hinges of any kind. It must have been done over since Bridget was here."

As if on cue, the little lady walked past us and right into the fireplace itself, whose top came just above her head. She ran her hands along the upper part of the right side, but nothing happened.

"Can you get me some light in here?" she asked.

I found a lamp with a long cord and plugged it into a socket that was close by. Brady put down the chair and picked up the lamp, turning it so that the light shone on the right-hand side of the fireplace. Bridget

THE BROKEN-HEARTED DETECTIVE

ran her hand along the top again, gave a little push and goddamn if the metal wall didn't swing in without a sound. Brady reached into the fireplace, lifted Bridget out of the way as quickly as he could, pulled out his gun and started to walk through the hole.

"Wait," I hollered, yanking my own gun from my waist with my right hand and grabbing his belt with the other. "Don't go barging in until we check it out. They could have booby-trapped it."

Vietnam must have raced through his mind because he stopped dead in his tracks. Then he carefully put his head around the corner for a look.

"Let me in there," said Daphne. "I know every trap in the arsenal. Let me check it out."

Brady, of course, didn't want a woman doing his work, but I tugged his belt hard enough for him to realize that it made sense. Daphne had been playing with these guys for years, and she knew the ropes. Maybe if she hadn't knocked him on his ass, he wouldn't have been able to understand how she might be able to do anything better than he could, but he'd remember that to his dying day, and he pulled back to let her past. She stuck her face exactly where his had been the moment before.

"There's a big room with a tunnel on the other side," she reported, "and one light hanging from a wall. It must get its power through a line from the house."

She felt around the frame of the opening with her hands, then the floor in front of her, and then popped through and was gone from my sight. Brady squeezed his way in behind her, and I was right after him, turning first to tell Betty and Bridget to stay where they were.

It was a big room all right, maybe forty feet square

with a ceiling about fifteen feet high. You could see where the hole had been drilled to snake through the wire for the light, and there were several broken bulbs underneath it. Scattered on the floor was everything from guns to cases of canned chili, but the most surprising thing of all was one of those electric golf carts.

Brady walked over and was reaching in toward the switch for the motor when Daphne yelled, "I told you not to touch anything, you utter fool." Utter fool. I liked that.

He pulled his hand out like he had touched hot metal. She came over and ran her fingers over the battery cover, and then lifted it up.

"Doesn't look like they wired anything," she concluded, reached in and turned the switch herself. Nothing. I could hear the air going out of Brady's lungs even louder than mine. When it came to disguises and knocking big men down, we knew that Daphne was a pro, but as far as explosives went, the jury was still out.

Suddenly, Daphne turned to her left and started to whip around the room with her head bent over like a dog sniffing a pissed-on area.

"Look," she said. "Look. There were at least three more of these vehicles here."

I could see faint outlines in the dust of the floor, but I never would have made a lab technician or an Indian scout so you couldn't prove by me that there had been three more electric golf carts parked in the area.

"The battery's dead," said Brady.

"What?"

"The battery's dead in this one. That's probably

THE BROKEN-HEARTED DETECTIVE

why they left it here. How far do you think it is to the end of that tunnel?"

I looked over at the black hole that was not quite six feet high and about seven feet wide. How far did it go? Far enough so that they used golf carts to go back and forth. Was there one tunnel or did it branch off into several? I walked over and looked into the blackness that led where? I could hear Brady coming from behind me when a man's voice called out, "What's going on in there?"

It was the manager of the resort whom we'd gotten to know during the search for my mother. He'd been as helpful as he could, but at the same time he had the look on his face that said "Why me? Why here? Why don't these people go away?"

"We think Reich and his bunch went out this way," I said, pointing to the tunnel.

"What is this room?" he asked, pushing his way through the fireplace. "There isn't supposed to be a room here. Mr. Reich didn't say anything about leaving. Do the police know anything about this? I don't understand what's going on."

His voice was getting higher and higher as he spoke, and you could sense the thousand worries that were flashing through his head about the home office, the guests, my mother's disappearance, the reporters, the whole schmear.

"We need a battery for this golf cart," said Brady, "and some flashlights and extra batteries."

"What?" said the manager, and for the first time he noticed the vehicle. "How did that get here?" He went over and looked at it. "It's not one of ours."

"But your battery will fit in here," said Brady, "and

we need it now. That guy took Vinnie's mother out through here, and we have to go after them."

Please, God, I said in my mind, let it be true. Let her be alive.

"I don't know," said the manager. "I don't know if . . ."

"Look, Mr. Renfrew," I told him, "the quicker we find my mother the quicker this place goes back to normal. We don't want to make a big stink; we just want to find my mother."

"But—" the manager began when Brady walked over and closed his big fist together on the manager's jacket so that he could bring him within a few inches of his face.

"We don't have time to argue," he said. "You get that cart battery and the flashlights here as soon as you can or you're going to be sorry you ever came to Arizona. Do you get me?"

The manager not only got him, but he also got the battery and flashlights. The two men who brought them down to us were so amazed by what they were seeing that they couldn't wait to leave to tell all their fellow workers so the battery was installed in no time, and we were ready to go.

While we had been waiting, I had been arguing with Betty about her coming along and even my being part of it.

"You've got to remember your condition," she kept saying to me. "Get the police to come back and do it. Let Brady go and find out what the situation is. Did you remember your pills?"

I finally took her by the shoulders and put my face as close to her as the manager's had been to Brady.

"Those bastards have my mother," I told her. "I

THE BROKEN-HEARTED DETECTIVE

know they do. I've got to go with Brady. You know I do. Staying here would be worse for me than anything that might happen out there. You told me not to be a cardiac cripple. This is the way I want to live as long as I can live. You're the one who gave me the guts in the first place. Don't try to take that away from me now."

She put her arms around my waist and pulled me tight.

"All right," she said, "but I'm going with you."

"No you're not," said Brady. "We can't be worrying about you while we're trying to do the job. No women."

"You wouldn't be talking to me, would you?" asked Daphne, strapping on a harness she had found on the floor and sticking the Glock into the holster. You could see the Beretta in her back pocket. Brady opened his mouth and then shut it again.

"Okay," I said to Betty, "you go find Petey and tell him what we're doing. Then call Sergeant Renzi and fill him in. I hope we'll be back before my brothers get here, but if not, tell Petey they're to sit tight until they hear from me. We can't have them barging into an unknown situation. They're not trained for this kind of thing. I hope we'll be back in a couple of hours with news, but don't panic. Brady and I have been down this road before."

She relaxed her arms enough to pull back a little and then she kissed me, a soft, loving kiss that added something extra to whatever the hell else we had going for us.

"Remember, Altobelli," she said. "Nobody dies on me. Nobody."

Brady was already behind the wheel of the golf cart, and Daphne was sitting beside him. I swung onto the back of the cart where the golf bags are usually stacked, and we were off. I was facing Betty and Bridget when we went into the tunnel, and they waved at me like you do when someone is going on a long trip, that slow, uncertain wave that shows you're not sure about the future. I didn't wave back.

28

Both Brady and I were worried about driving into the tunnel with the tiny headlights of the cart not only showing us the way, but also letting everybody else know we were coming. Daphne said it was the only way we could do it.

"They've already gone through," she said, "to wherever it is they go. First of all, they think that nobody else knows about the tunnel. They might leave a man behind to keep guard, but he would be at the end of the tunnel where he could camp out comfortably, not in the dark hole somewhere. It's possible he would see the light because anything is possible, but you have to figure the odds, and I'm certain nobody was left behind. There's nothing else but to do it."

The headlights were so weak that not even a glimmer carried back to where I was sitting, and it was like going on one of those rides at Disneyland where they take you through a dark tunnel before dropping you down a pit or turning you upside down. The only thing I thought about was my mother. Deep in my gut I knew that Reich had taken her, just as I knew why. He couldn't stand the thought of Betty preferring me to him and when he couldn't get her, he stole someone else I loved to even the score. Had he already killed her or was he keeping her so he could twist the knife in me some other way?

I felt the tears come into my eyes as I pictured my mother in the black in front of me, so strong but oh so small. Our house had always been like a hive of bees with the five of us continually buzzing around, but she filled the place with so much love and caring that nobody ever got stung. My father was content to let her run the circus, and that's what it seemed like sometimes with relatives and friends racing in and out all the time, and the smell of something good bubbling in a pot on the kitchen stove. When I was a kid, I was always worrying that my mother might die before me, leaving a hole in my life that I couldn't even imagine. But now she was sixty-six years old with a heart stronger than my damaged one, and yet this son of a bitch might already have taken her away from us.

It was impossible to slam on the brakes with a vehicle like this one, but Brady stopped so quickly that I fell over backward and banged my head on the iron bar where you hang the golf bags.

"Vinnie," said Brady softly, "there's daylight ahead."

He turned off the motor, and we all got out as quietly as we could.

"I'll go on ahead," whispered Daphne.

"We'll all go on ahead," I said. "If we run up

against anything, we want to use as much firepower as we've got."

Slowly, sticking as close to the sidewalls as possible, we made our way forward. The exit hole was a bit larger than the tunnel itself, and we finally reached the point where we could see each other plainly instead of just dark shadows.

"I'll check outside," said Daphne.

"You'll stay here with Vinnie while I check the outside," said Brady. Daphne was a take charge lady, or woman, as Carlotta had taught me to say, but Matt could take only so much. She didn't argue because she was smart enough to know that he well remembered her knocking him on his ass, and "THE END" had not yet flashed on the screen for that episode. We went into a crouch while Matt edged his way forward and then was out of the cave. I didn't realize I was holding my breath until he came back in and waved for us to come toward him. You could tell from the way he waved that there was nothing out there so we walked down the middle and out into the blinding sunlight.

We were in a tiny canyon that had sheer rock faces towering up toward the sky. Four golf carts were sitting just outside the cave exit, but there were no people in them. The rest was sand, nickel-size stones, a few small cactuses and no way out. Daphne went into her Groucho Marx imitation, running around in circles with her eyes focused on the ground.

"They left in some kind of vehicles," she yelled from across the circle, her voice echoing off the rock. "Probably jeeps or Land Rovers. This is where they went out."

We ran to where she was standing and saw a small cut in the rock where a vehicle could pass through. I

THE BROKEN-HEARTED DETECTIVE

moved through it and was in another canyon, a bigger one, this time with three cuts that you could go out from. I zipped through one of them and was in another canyon, this time with two exits. I was about to bolt through one of those when Daphne came tearing around the corner, yelling, "Wait! Wait! It's like a maze. You could disappear forever."

Strange about the desert. We couldn't be more than a couple of miles from the resort and less than twenty miles from Tucson, but for all that we could also have been on the moon without food or water or shelter. And if one of those sudden cloudbursts came up, we could also drown like rats.

"The ground is too hard," said Daphne. "I cannot track them beyond the next canyon. I don't know which way they went out of there."

"We've got to find them," I yelled. "We've got to find them soon. He's got my mother."

The echoes came back and hit me with "Mother, mother, mother, mother" ringing in my ears even as the sound died. Brady and Daphne were both looking at me funny, and it made me sad to see the pity in his eyes and the reality in hers. They both knew my mother was dead. I knew my mother was dead. But I was going to find her, and find her alive. She had to be alive. My mother had to be alive.

"Let's assess the situation," said Brady, walking over to stand beside me.

"Let's not waste time assessing," I said. "It will be dark soon, and then we'll be stuck."

"Use your head," said Daphne, moving beside Brady. "If we go blundering off into the canyons, we'll be lost inside of an hour, and we could die out here without water and food. At the least we'll need water.

We'll find them. I know we'll find them. But we have to plan the operation to give us the best probability. One of you will have to go back through the tunnel and get water."

"You go, Daphne," said Brady, "and Vinnie and I will keep looking."

"No," she said. "Be realistic. I am the only trained tracker among us. One of you will have to go, and the longer it takes to decide, the more time is wasted."

"I'm not going," I said, and without another word Brady turned and headed for our golf cart. If it had been his mother, I would have gone without saying a word. But it was my mother.

"Call the cops," I told him, "and ask for their help. And see if you can get hold of the FBI guys. They brought Betty to us to smoke him out, and they have to be standing somewhere in the wings. Do whatever the hell you can, and get back as soon as you can. Bring Petey back with you. Maybe there's a map of this area that will help us follow their trail. I don't know. Do what you can."

Brady disappeared into the tunnel without acknowledging even one of the things I told him. I turned and followed Daphne into the next canyon and checked one of the openings while she did another. There was no way I could tell if a vehicle had made tracks through there. I stood and stared into nothing when Daphne shouted from one of the other openings.

"Here," she yelled. "They went through here."

When I reached her, she was bending over a bush that had been flattened.

"See," she said. "It's trying to pull itself back up straight. They ran over it."

THE BROKEN-HEARTED DETECTIVE

"Let's go then," I said, starting to move through to the other canyon.

"Wait! We've got to make markers so we'll know where we've been and how to get back from false trails. Vincent, you're in no state of mind to handle this correctly. We can't afford to make a mistake in dealing with Kurt. Let me command the operation."

Even as she was saying it, I realized that she was right. Both my mind and stomach were churning, and I could fuck it up completely if I just ran around blindly. Daphne was making a small pyramid out of stones, and I gathered what I could to add to the pile.

She looked up at the sky and said, "It's going to be dark soon. We have to go back to the cave and wait for Brady to bring the water. At first light we can go all out."

Night comes so quickly in the desert. Once the sun sinks behind the mountains, the chill air settles down like a blanket, and everything is pitch-black until the moon and stars begin to make shadows.

Daphne leaned against the wall at the side of the cave entrance and sank slowly until her rear end hit ground. I did the same about three feet from her.

"I'm going to get some sleep," she said, "because we may have to go without it for a long period when we start the search tomorrow. I suggest you do the same."

She closed her eyes and in two seconds you could tell that she was sound asleep. I was sure that if even a dead cactus needle fell to the ground, she would snap awake and have the gun pointed at exactly the right spot. She was a pro all right. I was sure that even if it was her mother, she would still make herself sleep because that would be the correct thing to do.

I figured I wasn't a true professional because my mother's face never left the back of my eyes no matter what I was looking at. My throat got all tight and my eyes all wet. The rage was all gone from inside me, and I felt too weak to even stand up if I had to. What the hell was keeping Brady? I thought about walking back through the cave until I met up with him, but realized how stupid that would be even as I was thinking it. I had to be like Daphne if we were going to pull anything out of the mess. I had to concentrate so that all my training and all my energy and all my thinking would come together to free my mother and get that fucker Reich. But the cold feeling in my stomach wouldn't go away. It was still there when I fell asleep.

29

The rosy light through my eyelids came from the morning sun reflecting off the tops of the canyon wall, and startled awake, I rolled away from the stone, dragging out the gun as I came up on my knees. There was nobody there. No Daphne and no Brady.

Daphne! Where the hell was Daphne?

"Daphne," I yelled at the top of my lungs, not even thinking about anybody else hearing me.

There was no answer, and I ran to the opening that

THE BROKEN-HEARTED DETECTIVE

had the pyramid piled in the middle of it, and went through into the next canyon. On the other side I could see the bunch of stones laid down beside the plant that had now pulled itself all the way up again, and I went through that opening as fast as I could. Coming toward me was Daphne, and by the time we met in the middle I was so exhausted that I fell to my knees, my right hand covering a dull ache on the left side of my chest. Was my heart going to do Reich's job for him?

"I found another trail," said Daphne, seemingly unsurprised by my falling at her feet. "The sand gets softer after the next canyon, and the tire marks are visible."

I was having trouble just getting air into my lungs so I didn't say anything. My watch showed six-fifteen. What the hell had happened to Matt? It was more than ten hours.

"Brady's not back," I told her. "Something went wrong."

"We'll leave him a note," she said, "telling him that we've gone ahead, and he can find us by following the pyramids."

"What if something happened to him and he doesn't come? What about the water?"

She looked at me, surprise on her face.

"We can go a few days without water," she said. "Are you all right?"

"I'm all right," I told her, standing up. The pain had stopped but I was feeling a bit woozy, maybe from the heat, maybe from not having had anything to drink in twenty hours. "I'm all right," I said again. "Let's go back and leave the message. Have you got something to write with?"

She didn't and I didn't.

"You can scratch it in the sand or on a rock," she said. "You go back and do that, and I'll keep following the tracks."

"No," I said. "We'll both go back in case I need help in writing on whatever the hell else is available, and we should also stick together. If Brady isn't back soon, then both of us will go on."

She hesitated like she was going to give me an argument, then shrugged and took off for the home canyon without looking back at me. She set a hell of a pace, close to a trot, but I kept up with her. If she got to me this much just by walking fast, I could understand what Brady had gone through when she knocked him down. Where the hell was he? What had gone wrong?

As we jogged into our canyon, I looked around for a sandy spot where we could scribble a message, and as my eye passed over the mouth of the cave, the front of the golf wagon came into view. Brady was driving and Bridget Burns was sitting in the seat beside him, and Betty was perched in the back where I had been. I couldn't believe what I was seeing, but beyond that there was one of those garden carts attached to the golf wagon, and it was piled high with stuff. Daphne was as surprised as I was because she stopped dead in her tracks in front of me.

"Vin," yelled Brady, stopping the cart and squeezing out to the ground, "here we are."

"Why?" I shouted back. "Why the hell did you bring them into this mess? Are you crazy? Now we've got to worry about them too."

"They wouldn't let me go without them," he said, almost like a little kid claiming he hadn't done anything wrong. Here we were trying to hunt down a bunch of killers, and he had brought two more women to worry about.

"Altobelli," said Betty, advancing toward me while she was shaking some bottles in her hand, "you didn't take your medicine with you. Swallow these tablets right now."

She went back to the wagon behind the cart, opened a cooler and drew out a can of diet soda, which she handed to me along with the pill bottles.

"Take these right now," she said, "and then we're going to do your blood pressure."

Bridget Burns pulled a black bag like the ones doctors used to carry out of the cart, opened it, snaked out the blood pressure kit and advanced toward me while she was unwinding the cuff and slipping the stethoscope around her neck. I couldn't believe this was happening.

But seeing little Bridget reminded me of my mother, and the look on her face was the same one my mother wore when you had to take medicine or pick up the crap in your room or let my uncle Pietro hug and kiss you. I opened the ice-cold can of soda, extended my hand for the pills, and then held out my arm for the wrapping. She pumped and said, "One twenty over eighty. The man's a rock."

"Matt," I said, trying to be very calm so as not to raise my pressure, "would you tell me what the hell is going on? What took you so long? Why did you bring them? Are the cops coming? Did you reach Yert?"

"I brought them," he said, swinging his arm wide to include the two of them, "because they wouldn't take no for an answer. Betty said you needed her because of your heart condition, and Bridget has hiked in these canyons and can maybe save us some time."

"Is help coming?" I asked.

"The cops are out," he said disgustedly. "Sergeant Renzi's on vacation, and that Lieutenant Peterson hung up on me when I tried to push him on it. I'm going to pay that guy a visit before we leave town."

"What about Yert?"

"There's no such person. I called the FBI office and told them who I was and what it was about, and they put me on hold for about a half hour, and then the guy came back and said there was no such agent at that office. I had a feeling Yert was standing right next to him when he said it. That guy hung up on me too."

"Where's Petey?" I asked. "How come he isn't with you? Has he found a lead somewhere?"

Brady, Bridget and Betty exchanged looks at the same time, and Betty took two steps toward me with her right hand half lifted up. I felt my heart give a lurch but I couldn't talk.

"That's partly why I was so late," said Brady. "We were waiting to hear. Everybody's all right, but we had to wait to find out."

"Find out what, for Christ's sake?" I yelled at him. "Find out what?"

"Everybody's all right," he said again, "but your father and brothers mixed it up with a semi on the Interstate coming here, and they're all in the hospital in Bullhead City."

"Where the hell is Bullhead City?" I asked, walking up to him so that my nose was no more than an inch from his chin. "Why are they in the hospital?"

"They've all got something broken," he answered. "Your father and Dominic are in intensive care, but

Petey said their condition is stable, and your other brothers are already in regular rooms. We had to wait until he called back. They're all going to be okay, but they'll have to stay in the hospital while they check them out for internal injuries."

I stared up at the sun, feeling the burning glare blind me, when all of a sudden I felt two arms on my sides, shoving me around so that I was looking at Betty through a haze of dancing sparks.

I pushed her arms away, turned and started running for the canyon exit because I had to be alone, all alone, while I tried to figure out what was happening to me. *God,* I was saying to myself over and over, *what the fuck are you doing to me?*

I had gone through the second canyon when two small hands grabbed hold of my shoulders and twisted me to the ground. I hit a stone with my elbow that sent a shock of pain right through my skull, and I turned expecting to see Daphne standing over me because she was the only one who could have run fast enough to catch me. But it was Betty standing there, her chest heaving and the sweat running down her face. She dropped to her knees and took my face between her wet hands, pulling me maybe two inches from her own.

"Vinnie," she said, and there was something in her voice that made my stomach churn up in pain, "it's all my fault. If it wasn't for me, you and your whole family would still be in San Bernardino. It's all my fault. What have I done to you?"

Carlotta sprang right into my head right there in the middle of the desert. *If it weren't for me, Vincent,* she would be saying. Not *If it wasn't for me. If it weren't for me.* I looked over at Betty, the tears spurting out of her eyes like fountains do when they're set on a timer, my whole body reacting in a way that Carlotta the school teacher had never been able to spark, and I reached up my right hand and tried to brush her face clear, but she grabbed my wrist and pulled the palm into her cheek.

"I'm so sorry, Altobelli," she said. "I'm so sorry. Your mother. Your father and your brothers. All this." She swung her arm in a circle to take in the whole canyon.

"How did you catch me?" I asked her.

"What?"

"How did you catch me? I was moving pretty fast."

She looked at me strangely, wondering if there was more to my question than she was understanding.

"I was on the high school track team," she said. "Middle distance."

"Then it wouldn't do me any good to try and run away from you, would it?" I asked. "And even if you're faster, it wouldn't do you any good to try to run away from me. My mother always told us that everything has its purpose, and though this one is a son of a bitch to try to figure out, it will end up all right. You'll see."

"You think your mother's already dead, don't you?" she asked, and I felt the pain go right through me. I didn't answer.

"If that's the case," she said, "why don't we let the police or the FBI handle the rest of it? Those men want him dead, and eventually they'll get him. Why don't we go back through the cave and let them handle it?"

I had never felt calmer in my life. It was like God, or the Devil, had whispered in my ear.

THE BROKEN-HEARTED DETECTIVE

"No," I said, "I can't depend on anybody but me. There's still the chance she might be alive, and who knows when those pricks will decide to move on Reich. And besides, he owes me. He owes me his life now. The two of us can't live on the earth at the same time."

She was kissing my eyes shut when there was a yell, and the goddamndest caravan in the history of desert warfare came through the opening in the mountain wall.

30

Bridget was leading the pack, looking like one of those Irish elves you see in the cracker commercial except that she was striding away like she was seven feet tall. Daphne was driving the cart, and Brady was behind the garden wagon, pushing it every few steps because the little electric motor didn't have enough power to drag that much weight. They came up beside us and stopped, looking down at Betty cradling my head in her arms.

"You all right, Vin?" Brady asked.

"I'm all right," I answered, standing up as Betty dropped her hands.

"I took the batteries out of the other four carts," said Brady, pointing to where they were stacked in the wagon. "That should get us some distance until Bridget recognizes one of her landmarks."

"I've been through this area," Bridget muttered, and you could see she was wishing herself taller than the mountains so she could pick out the spot she wanted.

"Betty, you drive," said Daphne, climbing out. "We need someone light, but Bridget's legs are too short for the pedal. I'm going to follow the tracks they made, and I'll continue to leave stones as I go along. That way we can save time."

"I'll go with you," I said, "and then if you're not sure and there's more than one opening, we can check both of them out at the same time."

"Maybe Brady should do that and then you can drive," said Betty.

"No," said Brady, "it's better I stay with the wagon in case it has to be pushed along. It wouldn't be good for Vinnie to have to do that."

Would I ever get over that flash of anger that came every time somebody said I shouldn't do something because of my heart? It was like the tape was caught, and I was hearing the same thing over and over again. Brady meant well; they all meant well. But I didn't want to live like that. What made it even worse was that I realized I had to, so without looking at anybody I started off ahead of Daphne, almost jogging, waiting to hear Betty yell that I should slow down, but she didn't say a word. Daphne didn't try to pass me so I led the way into the next canyon, able to see enough of the tracks to go in a straight line.

That was how the day went, with the marks leading us to other openings when we were lucky and disappearing when the stones were too thick or when the wind had blown sand over them. Then we would have to check all the breaks in the wall until we came to the tracks again. Sometimes Daphne would take over the lead, and I would let her run ahead, saving my strength. It was boiling hot and we had taken off without thinking about water, and just when I reached the point where I couldn't make my throat swallow anymore, Daphne came back from the next canyon and said we should sit in the shade of a wall until the others caught up. There was no argument from me.

I was asleep before they came through about an hour later, and didn't wake until I heard them ask Daphne if I was all right.

"I'm fine," I said, standing up and waiting as Betty came toward me with the pill bottles and another can of soda. This time it was warm, but the fact that it was wet was enough to keep me swallowing until it was all gone.

Lunch for me was a bagel, a chunk of cheddar cheese, another can of soda and two plums for dessert.

"We grabbed whatever we could out of the kitchen," said Betty. "The manager was real nice about it. He looked terrible. Said he hoped we'd find your mother all right, and that this whole thing will be over and done with for good."

"We're on our second battery," said Brady. "That's why we were so far behind you. It's a mixed blessing. Each time we throw away a battery the load gets lighter, but then we don't have that much reserve power. Bridget says she has an idea where we are in general but not in particular. What do you think, Daphne?"

"We're doing maybe five miles an hour," she said, "and they're probably averaging between twenty-five and thirty so if his house isn't close by, we could run out of everything before we get to where they might have gone."

"Have people died out here without anybody knowing about it?" asked Betty. She looked pale under the tan she had picked up at the pool, and there was dirt smudged on the right cheek of her face. We all looked kind of beat-up what with the days of searching for my mother and not enough sleep. Even Brady didn't have his usual zip. I wondered how my father and brothers were doing in the hospital, and a chill went through me so I moved out of the shadow of the rock into the sun.

"It has happened," said Bridget, "but I can't remember when the last time was. People get lost out here every year, sometimes they break a leg or something, but they have a volunteer rescue team that goes out, and there are the Civil Patrol planes and they always find them."

"We sure haven't seen anybody," said Brady.

"That's how it is in this area," said Bridget. "There could be people in the next canyon to you, and you'd never know it."

"We'd better get going," I said. "There won't be that much daylight left."

We kept moving until just before dark, and to me the tracks looked fresher, but Daphne said she couldn't be sure, that maybe I was just wishing them fresher.

"We've got to find them, Daphne," I told her. "We've got to find them soon."

She didn't say anything, just took the kerchief off my head, soaked it with water from her bottle, and then tied it on my head again.

THE BROKEN-HEARTED DETECTIVE

"I'll smell them when we get close," she said. "I'll know."

"We'd better get going," I said, starting to push my way up from the rock.

"Sit," she commanded, like she might have been talking to a dog. "We've done enough for today. When the others come up, we'll make camp."

"You don't have to stop on account of me," I said, my voice going higher than I wanted it to. "I can keep up with you. You don't have to treat me like I'm an invalid."

She gave me a long look, measuring me.

"You're the one who's acting like an invalid," she said. "We're a team, and a team is only as strong as its weakest member, which you'll have to admit is probably you. When the time comes, if you're too weak or sick to do your part of the job, we could all die. You look pretty good to me right now, but that's how we're going to want you. You're not the only one who's tired. We're all tired. Even me. So we wait here and get some rest tonight, and tomorrow we'll be able to go on at a good pace. But if you get sick, we're not going to leave you alone, so the whole mission will be endangered. You want your mother. I want Reich. Let's do what is best for both of us."

"I want Reich too," I said, my voice softer than I meant it to be. "Because of him my whole family has been torn to shreds. I want him bad."

"You promised," shouted Daphne, standing up and looming over me. "We made a deal. We got your woman back. Now you have to keep the other part of the bargain."

We must have looked peculiar when the others came around the bend and into our canyon because

Betty jammed on the brake and they all stood there staring at us.

"You're right," I said to Daphne. "He's yours. I'll keep my word. He's yours."

She turned and walked over to the wagon to help Brady push it over some stones, and they all started talking at the same time. Betty brought over the pill bottle again and some water because we had drunk all the soda. There were still two big jugs of water left, but we had automatically started rationing without saying anything about it. The rest of the cheese had gone bad, but there were some hard rolls and a jar of peanut butter, which made you thirsty, but nobody seemed hungry anyway so we were all finished by the time the sun went down behind the mountain.

It's amazing how cold it can get in the desert at night. I talked to a couple of guys, well, one of them was a girl, who had taken part in the Desert Storm operation against Iraq, and they said the sweat would freeze on their bodies like ice cubes when the sun went down. We had only a couple of hotel blankets in the wagon so there weren't enough to go around.

We were all sitting there in the pitch black because the moon wasn't high enough to give any light when Betty took charge of the sleeping arrangements.

"Look," she said, "we're going to have to share body heat. Vinnie and Bridget and I will curl up in one of the blankets, and Daphne and Brady can roll in the other. Any objections?"

"I won't be cold," said Daphne. "Brady can have the whole blanket."

"No, you take it," said Brady. "I never get cold."

"We're going to do just as I said," Betty ordered,

using her intensive care unit voice. "This isn't a pajama party, you know."

So that's how we settled down. We wanted to put Bridget between me and Betty, but she claimed she might suffocate so Betty came first on the left, then me, then Bridget, then Daphne and finally Brady on the right. We wrapped the two blankets around as best we could, but if someone moved an elbow or breathed too deeply, the edges came loose. None of us was smelling too good, but somehow that made things feel a little warmer. I had my arm lying across Betty's waist, but as soon as everybody was settled in, she took my hand and tucked it over her right breast. I pressed in slightly like I was answering something she had said, and then I fell asleep. It was not what you would call a restful night, what with Bridget getting up at some point to walk down the wall away from us to go to the toilet I guess, and then everybody having to get adjusted again, but we got through it, and at the first blink of daylight we all got up on our knees and stretched, trying to get the rock ache out of our bones.

"Everybody take a drink," said Daphne, "and then let's get going. We're going to push through a lot of canyons today."

31

We almost missed it. The sun was hitting our eyes as we came into the canyon, and the house was built into the cliff in such a way that you could barely distinguish it from the rock around it. But we all knew right away that this was what we were looking for.

"Get back," Daphne yelled. "Get back before they spot us."

The rest of us stared at each other for a few seconds, then turned and scampered behind the canyon wall. When we realized Betty was not with us, we all ran back, and there she was trying to turn the wheel of the golf cart, but it was stuck on a rock, and finally Brady and I had to push it from behind to get it moving. Daphne, who had stayed out of sight, was completely disgusted with us when we returned out of breath and sweating bullets.

"You call yourselves professionals," she snorted at me and Brady.

"We couldn't leave her out there," I said. "And maybe they didn't see us."

"How do we know it's that man's house in the first place?" asked Bridget.

We all stopped to consider that. What if it was somebody else's house out there in the middle of nowhere? Hell, there were enough rich nuts in the world who built palaces where you couldn't build houses. Maybe this was one of them. And maybe it wasn't a real house. Maybe it was deserted. The *maybes* started crowding one on top of the other as I stood there.

"Did anybody think to bring binoculars?" Daphne asked.

"No, not even you," Brady came back. He was pissed that we had acted like amateurs, including Daphne, who had been right up front when we came out of the canyon mouth, although she was acting like she had nothing to do with the whole business. She ignored both the remark and him.

"I'm going to take a better look," she said, moving to the edge of the wall and inching her head just enough so that her left eye was able to see what was out there. Everybody else sat down, and Betty brought me a pill, which I swigged down with about a shot glass of water. Despite our being careful, the jugs were almost empty. Whether or not that was Reich's house, we were going to have to get water from somewhere, and that seemed the most likely place. Daphne returned to our midst.

"It's too far to tell if anybody is there," she said, "but there is plenty of cover up to about three hundred feet of the base."

"How far is the house from here?" asked Bridget.

"About a half mile," answered Brady.

"It's a little more than that," said Daphne. She wanted to answer all the questions, and I was worried that in her eagerness to catch Reich she might do something to get my mother killed. I wasn't going to give up. That house was Reich's and my mother was in it. Alive!

"I can't understand why Frye isn't around here," said Brady. "I keep having the feeling that there's a hundred FBI and CIA palookas just over the horizon like in a John Wayne movie."

"We can't count on them," I told him. "They set this up for us to do their dirty work. I've got a feeling that somebody in Washington is not sure how to handle this, and until he makes up his mind, Frye and Yert and their people are going to stand on the sidelines and watch the game."

"But surely," said Bridget, "they'll come in if they know we're in trouble."

Everybody just looked at her.

"I think it's quite likely," I said, as much to get attention off her as anything, "that they have no idea where this house is. So we've got to pull it off alone. Brady and I will get as close as we can when it's dark, and in the morning we'll be able to see what the place is like close up."

"I'm going to be there with you," said Daphne, looking around like she would punch anybody who disagreed.

"I think it would be best if we continue sticking together and all go up there tonight," said Bridget. "Staying back here isn't going to make it any safer. If something goes wrong, we'll all be in the soup anyway."

Betty sided with her and finally we agreed it would be the best idea to stick together.

"Have either of you ever used any guns?" I asked Bridget and Betty.

Betty shook her head, but Bridget nodded and explained that she was a member of a woman's gun club when she had worked in San Antonio.

"The women down there carry guns in their purses like we do lipstick," she said, "and a bunch of us nurses thought it would be fun."

"Was it?" asked Betty.

"As a matter of fact, it was. And I got a fella out of it that I almost married."

We all stared at her. I felt bad that it had never occurred to me that Bridget might have had a "fella." Why the hell not?

"Let's give the extra guns to Betty and Bridget," I told Brady. "You teach Bridget how the Beretta works, and I'll practice with Betty."

Daphne did everything but snort her superiority as we sat down with the women and explained about the safety and loading and how to aim and fire.

"It ain't easy to pull the trigger on a person," Brady told Bridget, "but we're not dealing with the Rotary Club here."

Betty watched me closely as I showed her how the Glock worked, and then she repeated it perfectly, including the two-hand hold.

"Can I talk to you alone?" she asked as we stood up. Her face had a strange look on it, and I felt my heart give a hard beat as I followed her around a bend in the mountain.

When she turned to me, I could see tears rolling out of her eyes, and I put my arms around her and pulled her in tight, feeling the greasy wet of her sweat against my face and chest.

"I have a bad feeling," she whispered into the crook of my neck. "I don't want anybody to die, but we've got guns and they've got guns, and if anything happens to any of you, it will be my fault, all my fault."

"We've been through this already," I told her. "Things

happen because they happen. In grade school we read a poem on how because of the want of a nail a shoe was lost, et cetera, et cetera, until the whole goddamned world went down the tube. You never know today how what you do is going to affect tomorrow. Who knows why you were on duty when Reich came in? Maybe God arranged it because of some plan that we can't understand."

"Don't give me voodoo bullshit, Altobelli, when I'm hurting like this. God had nothing to do with my calling you."

"If you hadn't called me, we might never have seen each other again. How do you think our kids are going to feel about that?"

She pulled back her head and looked at me, then took my face in her hands and kissed me so hard that our teeth grated against each other.

"I got everybody into this," she said, "and I'll get everybody out of it."

By the time we got back, Daphne had organized everything for our nighttime move. She had drawn a map in the sand with all the big rocks and bushes and cactuses marked, and described how we were going to advance before the moon was high enough to light shadows. We split a box of low-salt Triscuits, and each of us got a swig from the last bottle. Then all of sudden Brady started to quote poetry in a fake English accent.

"You may drink of gin and beer when you're quartered safe out 'ere," he practically sang, standing up so that he loomed over us, "and you're sent to penny fights and Aldershot it. But when it comes to slaughter, you will do your work on water, and you'll lick the bloomin' boots of 'im that's got it."

"Kipling," said Betty. "Brady just recited Kipling."

THE BROKEN-HEARTED DETECTIVE

"We had to memorize that in grade school," he modestly admitted, "but it was burned into my head in Vietnam. We've got just enough, and I mean just enough, water to get us through tomorrow. But then we've got to get more one way or another, and the only place we've got is that house. We can maybe last a day or two without water, but then we won't be worth shit. So whether it's that guy Reich or whoever, we've got to get either access to or control of that house by the day after tomorrow at the latest."

For Brady that was almost a speech, and I would have voted for him if he was running for office. Nobody said anything and we all just sat there in the shade while the sun disappeared over the mountains and darkness began to settle down. Just before it became black, Daphne, who had been peeking around the corner for practically the whole afternoon, suddenly yelped in a way that wasn't like Daphne at all, "There are lights. Lights just came on over there."

32

It's a good thing it was dark because we all rushed around the cliff face and stood there pointing to windows and floodlights as though we'd never heard of electricity before. We even started shouting to each other until Daphne emitted a loud *ssshhh* that stopped our mouths.

"Sound carries in this terrain," she hissed, and my joyful feeling disappeared as I realized that the only new thing in the pot was that there were people in that house. We still didn't know if it was Reich or somebody else. And our situation hadn't improved one bit. If my mother was in there, she was still in there, and I still didn't know how we were going to get her out. My heart sank as I asked myself *What if she isn't in there? What do I do next?*

Daphne organized us into two pairs with herself as a rover. She seemed to automatically take charge, and when Brady didn't say anything, I let her run with the ball. After all, this was supposedly a game in which she knew all the rules, and if she did something stupid, then we could step in. At first she wanted Brady to team up with Bridget and Betty with me, but we finally decided it would be better if Brady and I worked together as we had for so many years on the police force. Betty and Bridget would be our rear guard, staying out of the way unless there was some kind of life or death situation where a backup was necessary.

We divided up everything we could carry—food, water, blankets—although there was hardly any of the first two left, and even the blankets seemed thinner than when we had started. The moon gave us just enough light to move forward without bumping into or falling over anything, and we finally reached the closest point to the house where there was still cover. Daphne put us way over on the left where there was a clump of cactus, and Bridget and Betty on the right behind a stand of some kind of desert bushes. She said she was going to be behind a big rock that was almost in the middle between us.

THE BROKEN-HEARTED DETECTIVE

Just before we all spread out I asked Daphne what the plan was. We weren't going to do any better hiding close up than we would twenty miles away.

"I know you're impatient," she said, "but we can't rush in until we have an idea of what we're rushing into. Tomorrow we'll observe and find out who's there, what the security is, and see if we can pick out any weak spots. Then tomorrow night we'll make our move. We've come this far; let's not throw it away now."

She scuttled off to her rock, and I moved out to the left side of the cactuses so I could check out the house. Brady had gone off somewhere, either to do what I was doing or to use the toilet facilities. Someone, probably Brady because of his service in Vietnam, had thought to throw a roll of toilet paper into the garden wagon, and we had divvied that up along with everything else. He was carrying our share.

The house was built on three levels, and there was a series of terraces coming down from the cliff to the desert floor. How the hell had the place been built? Did they send a convoy of trucks out here with all the stuff they would need, and the workers lived in tents until the job was over? My brother Dominic, who has his own construction company, told me that people built huge houses on the tops of mountains by using giant helicopters. There was a whole series of solar panels on one side of the roof, and there was a steady hum coming from somewhere on the lower level. It had to be a generator, and I wondered what the cost per gallon came to when the fuel had to be brought out from wherever.

The head and upper body of a man moved past a window on the second floor, but he was gone too quickly for me to see who he was. But in another couple of minutes he not only came back but stood where I could get a good look at him. It was one of Reich's guards all right, the one who had punched me in the kidney and brought me down. His face was burned into me, and I could feel the heat in my stomach as I watched him. If only my mother would pass by, but I wasn't sure even her head would show because the windows were more than halfway up the walls.

Brady came back in a crouch, dropped to his knees beside me, and uttered a really deep groan.

"Are you all right? What's the matter?"

"Cactus needles. They sneaked up and used my right cheek for a dart board."

"It's them," I told him.

"What?"

"It's Reich's bunch in the house. I saw one of them in a window."

"You're sure it was one of them?"

"It was the one clocked me in the kidney."

Brady let out a sigh. You can bet he would have recognized the one who punched him. That guy still had some dues to pay.

"I'm going up closer," I told him, "and see if I can get any angles on taking these guys."

"Why don't you let me do it?"

"Because you're so clumsy you'd probably ring the doorbell."

Brady didn't argue because he knew it was true. I was the one who had always squeezed through windows or rolled through doors or picked the locks. Subtlety was not one of Brady's major achievements.

Moving slowly so if anyone looked out they would

THE BROKEN-HEARTED DETECTIVE

see no more than a shadow of the moon, I worked my way to the bottom of the first terrace and slipped over the low wall. Reich was used to having guards posted around him so there had to be one somewhere. There was a small glow coming from the left side of the terrace, and I crawled there to peek quickly over the wall. The four jeeps were parked in a shallow cave that had been blasted out of the side of the mountain. The light was coming from a small bulb that was hung over a steel door. Steel. When I looked up at the front door, I could see that it was also steel. Steel and stone.

There were no windows on the first floor and those on the second and third floors had steel mesh over them. It would take a real professional effort to break into that house whether anybody was living there or not. It would be something to be lost in the desert without water and come upon the house, and find that there was no way you could get in to save your life.

But we had to get in to save my mother's life, and I had to find the way to do it. I started to crawl back to the center when an arm snaked around my neck, and I felt the point of a knife at the side of my throat.

"One sound," said a woman's voice, "and you're dead."

"For Christ's sake, Daphne," I groaned, much louder than I intended, "it's me, Vinnie."

The hand slackened and the knife point disappeared.

"What are you doing here?" she hissed. "I didn't say you could come here. Do you want to scuttle the operation?"

I let the anger work its way through me, knowing that if I uttered one word before the fury poured out through my toes, I would say or do something that could screw up the whole business.

"Daphne," I said softly, "I was a policeman for eleven years, one of the best, and both Brady and I know how to deal with situations like this. If it will get my mother out of there, you can be superboss of the whole schmear. I came here to find out as much as I could, and what possible ways there were to get into this fort."

"There are no ways," she hissed at me again. What kind of a snake was she? "I've checked the whole place out, and the only way we can work this is to either get them to come out, or for us to figure a way to get in. The doors are all steel, and they've got those steel things coming out of each window so you couldn't even get a ladder or a hook up there. They're not going to stay here forever, so we may have to wait until they try to leave."

"We're not going to wait," I told her. "We're going in there one way or another, and we're going to do it soon. The longer my mother's in there, the more things can happen to her."

Her silence told me what I didn't want to know. Daphne was positive my mother was dead. The thing that was ripping at my guts right then was that I knew Daphne couldn't care less whether my mother was dead or alive. All she wanted was Reich, and if my mother got lost by the wayside, we would be lucky if Daphne even shrugged. She was Reich's woman all right, and it wouldn't have taken much for me to have reached out and grabbed her by the throat except that she was one of the few things we had going for us,

THE BROKEN-HEARTED DETECTIVE

and she might have killed me the instant my fingers touched her skin.

"You go back to your position now," she finally said, "and I'll go back to mine. Tomorrow we'll observe their MO, and maybe we'll see something that will allow us to form a plan of action."

"Sure, Daphne," I whispered, and crawled back over the wall before going into a low crouch to make my way to our stand of cactus. Brady was sound asleep, his giant body curled up in a circle. He had stacked the blanket for me to use, but I unfolded it and dropped it over him. I pulled a deep breath of air into my lungs as I looked at him, as close to me as any of my brothers. Then I lay back and looked up at the stars, feeling so alone that I thought about moving over to where Betty and Bridget were. But they were probably asleep too, and they sure needed it. I was surprised that Betty hadn't brought my pills over. She'd been like a goddamned alarm clock ever since she'd caught up with me again. But I was so tired that I couldn't even lift my arm. Maybe four hundred feet from me my mama was being held a prisoner by one of the world's worst sons of bitches. And I didn't even have the strength to lift my arm.

33

My eyes snapped open as if somebody had flicked a switch, and there they all were in a semicircle, staring down at me. I don't know when I had fallen asleep, but it was deep enough so that the light hadn't waked me. One of them must have made some kind of noise to jar my eyes open. They were all in a half crouch around me—Brady, Bridget, Daphne—and they all—where was Betty?

"Where is she?" I asked, and the three of them looked at each other, uncertain as to who was going to do the explaining. I could feel my heart jump into high gear, and deep in my throat was a lump that felt like it was choking me.

"We don't know," said Bridget. "We can't find her."

I jumped to my feet so quickly that the dizziness almost knocked me down again, and Bridget reached up a hand to steady me.

"Hypotension," she said. We all looked at her.

"Low blood pressure," she explained. "When you get up too fast, the blood doesn't get to the brain in time."

"Who saw her last and when was that?" I asked.

"Me," answered Bridget. "It was cold and we put the blanket around both of us, and I fell asleep. I

THE BROKEN-HEARTED DETECTIVE

woke up at first light and the blanket had been tucked around me, but she was gone."

"You think she got up and put the blanket around you and then went somewhere?"

"She definitely had to. It was pushed in all around me, and that couldn't have happened if I'd just rolled in my sleep. No, she had to be the one to do it."

"How far have you looked?" I asked Brady.

"I scouted the whole area," said Daphne, "and there's no trace of her. There was no sign of a struggle or anybody being dragged."

I looked over at Brady and he just shook his head.

"She's somewhere," I said. "She might have gone to the john and stumbled and hit her head or wandered off. We've got to spread out and find her."

"We can't just go barging around here," said Daphne. "If we blow our cover, then Kurt will know we're here, and it's essential that we have the element of surprise. The only way we can—"

"*Altobelli,*" a strange, metallic voice yelled out, loud enough so that it sounded like God was calling me to judgment. It took only a second to realize that it was an amplified voice like from a police car, but for that moment my heart stopped.

"*Altobelli!*" the voice repeated, and we all realized that it was coming from the direction of the house behind the cactus stand.

"Don't move," Daphne commanded, and wiggled her way to a spot where she could peek between needles.

"It's Kurt," she reported. "He's standing in the doorway and he's holding Betty in front of him."

Not even thinking about it, I ran around the cactus and stood in the open. There she was all right with him behind her, one arm around her neck and the other holding a bullhorn. You could see by the twist in her face that the pressure was hurting her. I took a quick step forward and then stopped even quicker. No fast moves. He could break her neck like you'd squeeze an orange.

"Ah," he said, and even through the bullhorn you could make out the satisfaction he was feeling. "Mr. Altobelli. As you can see, I have a friend of yours here. But you couldn't have been very good friends because she came back to me of her own free will."

The anger went through me like an electric shock, but as I opened my mouth, I heard Brady curse behind me, and in the two seconds I listened to him I realized what had happened. Betty had gone there in the night in the hopes of trading herself for the rest of us. I could almost hear her telling him the deal. *Take me out of here, and I will do anything you say.* Not having ever dealt with creeps like Reich, she had no idea that he would just take her and do what he was doing. In hopes of saving us, she had handed him the whole fucking ball game.

"Brady," I said softly, "stay where you are."

Just as softly, he answered, "He's going to fix your clock."

"Our only hope is that you people can somehow pull us out," I said, holding my lips stiff like a ventriloquist.

"Tell your big friend to come out too," said Reich.

"I'm here alone," I yelled.

"What?"

"I'm here alone!"

"Let us not play any games. I know he's here with you. And if he doesn't come out, then this woman will suffer for it."

"There's nothing I can do about that," I yelled.

"He's not here. I'm alone. No matter what you do to her, nothing can change that."

This was maybe the biggest bluff of my life, but if Brady wasn't out there to do something for us, Betty would be broken into little pieces, and I would be dead.

Reich was silent and then pulled back from the door, both he and Betty disappearing. He was back in a few seconds, but this time he had to reach his arm down to hold the neck that was in front of him.

Mama!

God would not take a good woman like this before her time. Deep in my heart I had known she was alive, and I made the sign of the cross on my chest, and pledged a thousand novenas in gratitude for her safety.

Except that she still wasn't safe. Betty wasn't safe. I wasn't safe. None of us was safe until this crazy man was put away for good.

"Don't come out, Brady," I said softly between my gritted teeth. "You're our only hope."

"If the big man doesn't come out in the next minute, I'm going to break your mother's arm," the voice from the bullhorn said. It was so unreal coming out like that. Reich's way of talking was like it came from a computer to begin with, and the crackling noise made it even more like one of those *Terminator* movies.

Brady and I had been together long enough to know when a man was going to do what he said he was going to do, so all of a sudden he was standing beside me.

"That's better," said Reich. "That's much better. Where are your weapons?"

"We only have one," I shouted. Could it be that he did not know that Daphne and Bridget were also behind the thicket? What had Betty told him? She had probably told him nothing. She had probably told him that she had come alone, but of course he wouldn't have believed her. He knew I had to be along somewhere. And he knew that where I was, Brady would be. But he didn't seem to be aware of the women. Why would he?

"We have only one weapon," I yelled to him.

"If you are lying, I will hand you your mother's arm," the bullhorn threatened me.

"We have two," I conceded.

"That's better. You're beginning to understand the rules now. Altobelli, you get the guns. The other one stands right where he is."

I turned and went back behind the cactus. Reich didn't trust the safety of his men outside of the house so he was letting us do the work.

Daphne and Bridget were crouched down.

"He doesn't know we're here," said Daphne. "Do as he says and I will get you out."

"Me too," said Bridget.

I looked at the two women. Daphne was supposedly a pro, but there was no real way of knowing how good she was in a showdown. Bridget was a nurse, a very small nurse, and although she had belonged to a gun club in Texas, going against a bunch of thugs was not her field of expertise.

"The best thing you can do," I told them, "is hightail it back to the resort as quick as you can and get the police and the FBI in on this. They'll have to do something when you tell them the situation."

"You're right," said Daphne. "As soon as it's clear, we'll go back. It will be much quicker with the trail we marked. You've just got to hold on until we return."

"Isn't there something we can do?" asked Bridget.

"No," answered Daphne. "A good agent measures

THE BROKEN-HEARTED DETECTIVE

the situation and takes appropriate action. There are too many of them and their position is secure. We—"

"Altobelli," boomed the bullhorn, "you had better get back out here."

"Take the Berettas," said Daphne. "We'll keep the machine pistols."

I grabbed the Berettas by the barrels and walked back into the open beside Brady.

"Slide out the magazines," ordered Reich, "and let them fall to the ground."

I pressed the buttons on the two guns and the metal cylinders dropped to the sand from their own weight.

"Now each of you hold a gun between your teeth and walk toward me, keeping both hands at your sides."

"What the hell," Brady exploded, and Reich must have seen the look on his face even though he couldn't hear him at that distance.

"Do as I say, big man," he ordered, "or you'll be responsible for harm coming to your friend's mother."

It was all so formal, almost polite, and there was my mother standing there with that son of a bitch's arm around her throat, no expression on her face. The tears came into my eyes as I thought about the way she had taken care of all of us, always there, day or night, summer, winter, whatever, and I had to stand there while all it would take was one twist of his arm and she would be dead.

"Brady," I said, between my teeth, "grab the two guns and ammo and take off. Just make sure he pays for what he's going to do."

There was no doubt in my mind now that my mama and me were going to disappear, and the same thing would happen to Brady if he came along.

"They've got rifles on us from the upper windows,"

said Brady, "and if they're any kind of shooters, we're dead before two steps."

He reached out, took one of the Berettas, and put it between his teeth. I did the same.

"Now walk to the house," came the order again.

It took us a few minutes to reach there, and as we got closer, I could see the guns sticking out of the upstairs windows. We started up the first terrace, and Reich pulled my mother back through the doorway. Coming in from the bright sun, it took some seconds to adjust to the lack of light, but I finally made out Reich standing in the middle of a large hallway, still holding my mother around the neck, and three of his goons spread out to cover us with their guns.

"Well," said Reich, "it's time for the big reunion scene." And he threw my mother against the wall nearest me so that her body smashed into the brick and her head banged against it, and she slid to the floor into a tiny heap.

34

Brady and I went for the son of a bitch at the same instant, throwing ourselves across the room like we were shit-seeking missiles. The guy to the left of me swung his arm in exactly the right arc to put the stock of his Uzi across the back of my skull, and my mother, the room and Reich's smiling face disappeared.

THE BROKEN-HEARTED DETECTIVE

The only other times in my life that I went all the way out were during a high school football game when two guys blindsided me, and when I had my heart attack. The first face I saw when I came to at the football game was that of my coach, Doug Harlan; the first face at the hospital was Betty's; and when I opened my eyes this time, it was my mother looking down at me. She was sitting on the floor with her legs crossed, holding my head in her arms and dripping tears on my face. I was lying straight out and Brady was leaning against the wall opposite me, the left side of his face covered with blood.

"Vincent," my mother was crooning to me just like she did when in the fifth grade I had the fever that went up to a hundred and four degrees, and she spent the whole night sponging me off with alcohol. I lifted my hand and felt the lump on the back of my head, but there was no sogginess from blood. Brady hadn't been so lucky.

"Are you all right, Ma?" I asked her.

"Matty," she said, her voice cracking, "he's awake."

Brady didn't bother to answer, but he leaned forward away from the wall, rolled to his knees and got to his feet.

"You all right, Matt?" I asked stupidly. He should of told me it only hurt when he laughed, but he just nodded his head and put his hand on the adobe to steady himself.

I glanced up at my mother, who looked so tired that my hands squeezed into fists, and I shoved myself up on my elbows. She always had circles under her eyes, but these were so deep that you could have shelved a dime inside them. And there was a grayness to her face that sent alarms running through my brain.

"Are you all right, Ma?" I asked again.

"Who are these men, Vincent?" she asked. "Why are they doing these things?"

My mother once explained to me, when the patrol car brought me home from our farewell high school beer keg party in Woodlawn Park, the difference between good and bad boys. She had seen her share of both what with five hell-raisers to contend with over the years, but we had all turned out pretty well so what she had told us and the way she and my father lived had made a difference.

But what could I tell her about Reich and his pack of killers? She knew nothing about the CIA and the crap they pulled in the name of life, liberty and the pursuit of money. When you came right down to it, I knew nothing about it. But if a man like Reich could be one of their policymakers over the years, there had to be something very wrong with the whole schmear.

But before I could think of anything to tell her, the door opened and Betty was pushed into the room by somebody I couldn't see before it was slammed and locked again. She came over and knelt down beside us, her right hand reaching out to my left wrist. Christ, she was taking my pulse.

"Are you all right?" she asked.

That was hands down the question of the day. Nobody else had answered it so I went along with the custom. I sat all the way up, expecting my head to explode but there was only a dull ache.

"He didn't keep his word," she said, grabbing my wrist with both hands. "He said he would leave you all alone, but he didn't keep his word. The reason I—"

"I know," I told her. "I know why you did it. Now we have to take it from where we are."

THE BROKEN-HEARTED DETECTIVE

I must admit that underneath all my loving understanding there was this fierce urge to scream that she had done a very stupid thing, that she had made things worse, that anybody with half a brain would have realized that you can give a guy like Reich nothing, that you can trust him as far as you could move one of the mountains outside, that she was the one who had started the whole mess and right then my feeling for her was on very shaky ground, and that if it came to her or my mother, it was no contest. But that would have been stupid and gained us nothing, and as I looked at her beautiful face, I realized that in the long run she was worth whatever damage had been caused.

"Why did they put you in here?" Brady sensibly asked.

"He told me to tell you that he needed answers to some questions, and that the interrogations would begin shortly," she said, and I could hear his voice exactly as he had given her instructions.

"What are they doing now?" I asked.

"He's been on the telephone all day ..."

"What telephone?" asked Brady.

"One of those telephones you carry in a briefcase," she said. "Some of the doctors have them."

"We know about those," I told her. "Who is he talking to?"

"He's trying to get through to someone in Washington, but they keep telling him the man is unavailable. He got so mad he threw the phone against the wall and broke it."

"Broke it?"

"He's got two more of them."

The door opened and Reich's nephew Terry came in. Standing behind him was a guy with a grease gun. The kid's face was all red, and he tried not to look anybody in the eyes.

"He wants you," he said, pointing at me. "He wants to talk to you."

Brady moved between us and stood there.

"Maybe he should talk to both of us," he said.

The kid looked around at the guard who raised his gun at the same time he shook his head no.

"Just him," the kid said, pointing around Brady with his finger.

"Stay alive, Matt," I said, and moved around him to the door. "Just stay alive."

35

Reich was using his cellular phone when the punk shoved me through the door. Terry had not looked at me once as we came down the hall. I thought about saying something to him, but wasn't sure which tack to take so I let bad enough alone.

"Listen, you stupid, grade seventeen piece of shit," Reich yelled. "You tell the big boss he's got twelve hours to get back to me, and I don't care if he's at Camp David or on the moon. This is my final warning. I will not be calling again."

As he clicked off, he looked like he was going to throw this phone at the wall too, but he was too smart

THE BROKEN-HEARTED DETECTIVE

to burn all his communication bridges no matter how pissed he might be. And he was pissed. When he looked over at me, I could tell that he was thinking about how much pleasure he would get by hurting me. My old girlfriend, Carlotta, the schoolteacher who sometimes treated me like one of her high school students, had made me read a book on the history of torture one time when she was all concerned about police brutality. It was the kind of stuff you never get out of your mind, that you dream about sometimes, and it did change the way I handled perps for a while. Then one day a young punk tried to knife me with a blade he had hidden in his hat, and I kicked the shit out of him without even thinking about his being a fellow human in my total power. Brady took the occasion to welcome me back to the real world.

"Bring him over here," Reich said, and I was shoved to within three feet of him. He stared at my face for what had to be a whole minute like he was a doctor getting me ready for plastic surgery, and figuring out what I would look like when he got through. That examination of his went all the way to my belly.

"Altobelli," he said, "strange developments have taken place since you entered my life. There has to be a connection somewhere, something you have done, something you have said, something that you know, maybe someone that you know. Now I need to know what that something is. As a person who has participated in interrogations, you are aware that they can be handled many ways. The classic one is good-guy, bad-guy. I myself took part in such techniques in my younger days."

He smiled.

"I was always the bad guy," he said.

I don't know how I was able to do it because I was scared, but I smiled back, soft and friendly, like I appreciated his humor. From the way he braced I thought he was going to hit me, but he was still too much in control to do something like that when he was working out an interrogation MO.

"Ah," he said. "You find this amusing. That's good. That's very good. Now let me tell you something that may make you die laughing. I want to know what happened between you and Stevens when he kidnapped you from my quarters."

Stevens? Kidnapped? It took me a few seconds to make the connection. The CIA guy. The one who pulled me out when Reich was about to permanently alter my face and probably my life.

"We said good-bye when he and his men turned off at the parking lot, and that's all that happened."

"Come now," he said, "I told you this was serious. What did you do that got Washington to pull Stevens and his men out? Who is your contact in Washington? Is it the president? Do you have something on the president himself? What is the connection?"

I decided to go all the way in hopes that what I was about to tell him would be factual enough to maybe hold him back a bit.

"I have met Northrup Frye and Robert Yert," I began.

"Who is Yert?"

"He is an FBI agent who seems to be working with Frye. It was the FBI that was holding Betty until they gave her back to me."

"What do you mean holding her?"

"They had her out at some ranch in protective cus-

THE BROKEN-HEARTED DETECTIVE

tody. It had something to do with you, but they never told me why."

"Why are you telling me all this?" he asked, his face puzzled.

"Because I don't want to get worked over while you try to get me to tell it, and also because even though I don't know it for a fact, I feel that these guys are somewhere around here, and they are eventually going to catch up with you. If you have dead bodies on your hands, and that includes ones that have been buried somewhere in the desert, or cemented up in a cave, or maybe just people beaten to a pulp, they're going to make you pay for it no matter how much clout you think you have. Why is that guy in Washington dodging your calls? Is it because they're getting ready to make a move on you, and they don't care anymore what kind of tapes you have to use against them?"

He slapped me hard on the side of my face, and the guy behind me stuck his gun into my backbone in case I had an idea of trying to swing back.

"How do you know about tapes?" asked Reich, his face all red.

The last thing I was going to mention was that Daphne was floating around out there somewhere.

"Frye told me. He said he thought you were bluffing, but they were going to check it out."

"They know I'm not bluffing," Reich yelled. "I played them the tape of my discussion with the director. They are not fools. There is something else going on, and you know what it is, and you are going to tell me about it."

"I'm telling you all I know," I said. "You can pound me into dust, but I can't tell you more than I know."

"Don't you think I know when someone is lying?" yelled Reich, hauling off and belting me across the face again. Even though the guy still had his gun stuck in my back, I swung anyway and caught Reich smack on his left ear. I don't know how much the wallop hurt him, but getting hit just right on the ear can sting like a bee hive, and he staggered two steps to the side. What kept the guy behind me from pulling the trigger I don't know. Maybe he didn't blast anybody until he got the order, but my stomach was tight as a drum as I waited for the shock of the bullet to smash into my spine. When nothing happened, I took a quick look and saw that the guy's eyes were on Reich. He was going to do only what Reich wanted him to do. So I took a quicker look at Reich, and he was standing there stiff as a board, his eyes staring at my face like the vampire in one of those horror movies.

"Terry," he said, his voice so even that it could have been a recording, "go get Altobelli's mother."

I knew instantly what he had in mind, and I went for him with both arms swinging, but he danced out of my way, and as he moved, he shot his clenched right fist straight into my solar plexus. I went down like one of those NASA rockets that's out of control, unable to breathe and with a pain that made my heart attack seem like it had been a tickle. I wasn't unconscious but I had no control over any part of my body, and all I could think of was getting some air into my lungs.

Reich stood directly over me, looking down like I was something creepy or crawly, and he wanted me dead but he didn't want to mess his shoe by stepping on me.

"Altobelli," he said softly, and at least my ears were

still working. "Listen to me, Altobelli. You embarrass me. When I think of the people I have gone against in the past twenty-five years, gone against and triumphed over, I am shamed to think that I have let someone like you make me give more than a moment's notice. But that's over now. You are dealing with Reich, man. Kurt Reich. The indecision is over. Washington will pay in its time, but you are going to pay right now. Move one muscle and I will kick you in the face. Or I will have Stephen put bullets in you that will cause irreparable damage and pain, but will not make you unconscious. Are you getting the picture?"

He turned and shouted in the direction of the doorway.

"I ordered you to get the old lady," he yelled. "Why are you still standing there?"

It had to be Terry who hadn't done what he'd been told to do, but I didn't have the strength to turn my head to look. I was able to manage shallow breaths, but nothing more. He had squeezed his hand into one of those karate fists, and it had felt like a ramrod going into me. Score one for karate over the Mike Tyson approach. I didn't know where the guy with the gun was, but he couldn't have been too far away, and nobody said a word until suddenly I saw Terry handing my mother over to Reich. I tried to shove myself up, but the guy behind me put his foot on my upper arm, and I wasn't able to push it off. The pain was easing in my belly, but there was no strength in my entire body.

Reich took my mother's right arm and twisted it up behind her back. She hadn't said a word when she came into the room, and her face didn't change a bit even though I could tell that he had the arm high enough to really hurt. Her bones were small, and it wouldn't take much to make her whole shoulder snap out of place. Tears filled my eyes until I could barely see, but when I opened my mouth, the guy took his shoe off my arm and jammed it into my throat.

"All right, Altobelli," said Reich. "I'm about to ask you a series of questions. If you choose not to answer or if you answer and the answer doesn't, in my judgment, sound truthful, I am going to break your mother's arm. It's a matter of how much you make me want to believe you. Now the first question is—"

The explosion was so powerful that the whole room shook, and a great white light passed through the room like a shock wave from an atomic blast, and the foot went away from my throat, and Reich dropped my mother's arm, and they all ran toward the door.

"What the hell was that?" Reich was screaming. "What happened?"

"The jeeps," somebody yelled back. "The jeeps just blew up."

"Daphne," I whispered to myself as I rolled over on my side and started to push up on my knees. "Daphne, you fucking marvel, you."

36

Reich had thrown my mother aside when he ran out of the room, and I crawled on my hands and knees to where she had fallen on the floor. Her eyes were open, and I could see her chest moving up and down, but she didn't answer me when I asked her if she was all right.

"Ma," I repeated, "are you all right? Talk to me, Ma."

Her eyes were filled with tears, and she let out a short snuffle sound, but she wasn't able to say any words. This was a tiger who had been protected all her life, first by a loving husband, and then by five large sons who handled her like she was the porcelain statue of Jesus on the cross that she so proudly exhibited in the middle of the dining room table. My aunt Clara had brought it to her when she had visited us from Italy when I was twelve years old, and my mother was convinced it was an ancient work of art. Which it could have been because my cousin Rodolfo, Clara's son, was a capo or something like that in the Sicilian Mafia. I have never met him, but my brother Dominic did once, and he said Rodolfo has eyes like a fish.

But now my mother was down on the floor with me, neither of us strong enough to stand up, and I started thinking about what my brothers would do to me if they saw her in this condition. Christ, my brothers. They and my father were in the hospital, and all of it, the whole thing, was because they were trying to help me. For one of those nanoseconds that they're always talking about on "Star Trek," I wished that I had never met Betty Wade, that it had been another nurse, the older one, who had seen me through in intensive care that first time.

I got so angry—at me, at them, at the whole fucking world—that I shoved myself to my feet, and then pulled my mother up beside me. There was still a lot of yelling going on somewhere in the house, but we couldn't just stay there and wait for Reich to come back and continue where he had left off.

"Come on, Ma," I said, putting my arm around her and leading her out of the room into the long hallway. We moved down to the end, and on the right was a kitchen with something cooking on the stove, but nobody there to watch the pot. There was a door to the outside, which had some kind of fancy apparatus on it with bolts and bars and a chain around the bars with a lock on it, but beside it was another door, which turned out to be the way to the bottom floor. I knew I'd never be able to undo the locking crap before someone came in so I led my mother down the stairs, which had a generator going and a fuel tank beside it, and a large boiler and several packing crates behind them.

I could hear voices from the kitchen area so I led my mother over to the packing cases, thinking to hide behind them for the moment, but when we got there, I saw that one of them had been pried open, and the inside was big enough to hold the two of us. I carefully

THE BROKEN-HEARTED DETECTIVE

pushed my mother into the darkness and started to go in after her, but I stopped halfway through. What was I going to do? Sit there in hopes that somebody would rescue us? Sit there until Reich found us? No, I had to go back up there and get a gun and bust Brady and Betty loose and end this shit once and for all.

"Ma," I said, "I have to go back upstairs. I want you to stay in this box until I come back for you. You have to stay very still and not make any noise. Will you do that, Ma?"

She didn't say anything, and when I looked at her face, I saw that the tears were still falling from her eyes, and there was a grayness to her skin that made a shiver go through me.

"Everything's going to be all right, Ma," I said. "Everything's going to be all right. You just have to stay here for a little while, and then everything will be all right."

She reached out both hands, the brown spots on the backs standing out so big against the whiteness of her skin, and grabbed hold of my right arm, clamping on so hard that I could feel the fingers biting into my skin. I thought for a second about taking her with me, but realized how foolish that would be. These guys were too good at their game to give them any kind of an edge, and if she were with me, my attention would be very divided.

I reached up and pulled her hands apart, slowly at first because I didn't want to hurt her, but hard enough to do the job. I could feel the tears forming in my own eyes.

"Ma," I said, "you have to be brave just the way you told me to be brave when I got the big sliver in my stomach. You have to stay here while I take care of things. If you're with me, it's going to make it a lot tougher. Everything's going to be all right."

"Vinnie," she said, "your heart. You have to be careful of your heart."

She talked. My heart gave a big leap when I heard her voice again.

"My heart's fine, Ma," I told her. "My heart's big enough to handle these guys. But you've got to stay here."

She nodded and settled down on the bottom of the crate. I bent over and kissed her on the top of her gray hair, turned and went up the stairs, my ears cocked for any sounds. There was shouting coming from somewhere, but it was muffled. I took a quick peek around the doorway into the hall. Empty. I eased into the corridor and started toward where I thought Brady and Betty were being kept when out of nowhere a guy came around the corner and stopped dead when he saw me. He had a gun in his hand and raised it straight out in front of him so that it was pointing right at my belly.

"You stop right there," he ordered, and I stopped. It was Terry, Reich's nephew, and I could see his hand shake as it tried to hold the gun steady. This guy wasn't a trained killer like the others. He was there because Reich was doing his sister a favor. Would he have the guts to shoot anybody? I looked into his face, trying to read whatever the hell might be there, and what I read was fear. He had a gun and I didn't. He had the drop on me, but he was the one who was shaking. Would he be able to pull the trigger?

"Terry," I said, "you're in over your head. You still have a chance to come out of it if you don't do any-

THE BROKEN-HEARTED DETECTIVE

thing wrong. I'll vouch for you with the authorities. I'll tell them you had nothing to do with the bad stuff, and that you helped when the chips were down."

As I was talking, I was walking slowly toward him, a half step at a time, my eyes never leaving his. Two more steps and it would be jumping distance.

"Stop right there," he said, "or I'll shoot."

I moved another half step closer, and then I saw him close his eyes, and I dropped to the floor as the bullet whizzed by my head and left a burning in my left ear. I put my hand up and touched the ear, and it came away all red. He'd winged me in the ear. He didn't know where the hell he was shooting with his eyes closed, but he'd shot me in the ear, a half inch from my skull. He was standing there now with his eyes open again and the gun hanging straight down because his arm didn't have the strength to hold it. But just as I reached him to take it away, Reich yelled from behind me.

"Touch that weapon," he roared, "and you're dead on the spot."

I couldn't take the chance of trying to grab the gun from Terry and then whipping around and shooting. So I stopped still and waited for the orders.

"Turn around slowly," said Reich, "and don't even twitch."

I turned and he was standing there with an Uzi trained on my belly, ready to stitch me up good. Beside him was Twining, his underboss. He was holding a gun with a long barrel, a kind I had never seen before. It looked like it could blow a hole through an elephant.

"Where's your mother?" asked Reich.

"I left her in the room," I told him.

"Then let's go back to the room and see how she is," he said, and there was something in his voice that made me want to scream his name and go for him right there even when he had the fucking piece square on me. But my mother was down in the cellar, and it wouldn't do her any good if Reich cut me down in the hall.

The room was empty, of course, when we got there, and Reich turned on me in a fury.

"Where is she?" he demanded.

"She couldn't move," I told him. "She was lying on the floor when I ran out in the hall. One of your people must have taken her someplace."

"My people," he said, his voice changing to deadly calm, "have too many other things to do than babysit your mother. If you don't tell us where she is, it will go doubly hard on her when we find her. You don't want your mother hurt, do you?"

"You know I don't, you son of a bitch," I told him, "but I have no idea where she is. I am holding you responsible for the safety and welfare of my mother, and you've already got more trouble than you can handle right now."

"There is nothing I can't handle," he sneered, "but I do need some information. Who was out there to blow up the jeeps?"

"How should I know?" I answered. "I'm in here. Maybe it's the CIA. Or the FBI. Or both. Maybe it was one of your own men. Did you ever think of that? Maybe one of your guys is playing both ends against the middle. Like what's-his-name here."

Twining walked over and smacked me in the face, one of those cupped-hand hits that makes your head ring. How many times had I given the same response to some punk who was wising off? Sometimes you had to wonder about God's sense of humor.

"Russell," commanded Reich, "go get the big one and the girl and bring them here."

After he left the room, I decided to take a shot at it.

"Look," I said to Reich, "all you're doing is digging your hole deeper. You've got nothing to gain by holding us. There's somebody out there, and we both know it's probably the government men. For some reason they're not afraid of you anymore, of your tapes and your videos and your memos, or whatever else you were holding over their heads. I don't know how many counts they have against you now, but if something happens to us, they'll be able to put you away on charges that have nothing to do with whatever the hell the government doesn't want to get in the papers. Use your head, man. All we want is to get the hell out of here. If you let us go, that's the last you'll ever hear of us. All we want to do is go home and get on with our lives."

"The woman must pay," he said.

Woman? What woman? Betty! She had rejected him, and he couldn't let go of it. I looked at his face, and there was craziness there, craziness that had nothing to do with what had happened to him in the CIA or with Betty. The man was alone in a world of his own, and there was no way anybody was going to reason him out of anything. It had come down to kill or be killed, and as I thought of my mother in the cellar and Betty and Brady, I knew that I could do it if the chance presented itself. Even if there was no chance, it had to be done, and I could feel my muscles tense as I readied for a leap at him when Brady and Betty came through the door.

Brady was holding his hands behind his back and when he turned a bit, I could see that they had put a pair of nylon handcuffs on him. They hadn't secured Betty, but from the way she was standing, I could tell that she didn't have much left in her.

"Betty," I said. "Nobody dies on me. Nobody."

She looked over at me as if she had just waked up from a nap, and she smiled, a real smile, and I smiled back at her.

"Very touching," said Reich. "Very touching. Now listen to my plans, and we'll see if you smile over those. Russell, I am going to take the woman up to my bedroom. When I am through with her, she's yours. And then any of the other men who might want her. If any of these people as much as smiles again, they are to be shot immediately. Shoot them where they won't die. Shoot them where they will live for a while. I will call for you shortly."

As he turned and reached out his arm to grab Betty, his boy Russell was shoved so hard from behind that he went all the way across the room and smashed into the wall. And while our eyes were following his progress, Daphne leaped into the room with her gun pointing at Reich.

"Kurt," she yelled, "your time has come."

But before she could take any satisfaction out of getting the drop on him, the guy went into action so fast that he made Daphne's takedown of Brady look like slow motion. He whirled through the air, his left foot catching her in the jaw, his right foot kicking into her stomach, and she went backward into the wall as hard as Russell had done on the other side, and her eyes were glazed as she slid to the floor and lay there like a pile of rags. The teacher still knew more than the pupil.

Before I could move, Reich had turned back and his gun was pointing right at me.

"Things are starting to pull together now," he said, as though we had been discussing the weather. "She and I blew up fifteen of Noriega's jeeps the same way. There is no CIA or FBI out there. There was only this foolish woman. Now we can get down to business."

He lifted his gun toward me, and I froze as I waited for the bullet to hit, unable to jump or run or fall down. But before he could pull the trigger, a tiny figure came whirling through the door yelling *"Freeze"* at the top of her lungs. And there was Bridget with an Uzi cradled in her arms come to rescue the big people.

37

He stitched her with bullets from her forehead down to her crotch, the Uzi spitting death so quickly that her body didn't have time to fall until the last bullet entered. I heard Brady scream like one of those bull elephants in a Tarzan movie, and it triggered my body toward Reich in one gigantic leap.

I hit him with all my hundred and seventy pounds in the air, and drove him back against the wall so hard that the gun was knocked from his hands, and I was pummeling at him even as we slid to the floor where I felt his hands go around my throat and start to squeeze, the thumbs pressing into my windpipe. I tried forcing his arms apart but it was like trying to bend iron so I reached down, grabbed his nuts in my right hand and tried to yank them off right through his pants.

The hands left my throat to grab my arm, but I held on for dear life because I could feel my heart racing so fast that I knew at any moment it could give out, the damaged part unable to handle the demand that was being put on it. Brady screamed again just as somebody grabbed me by the hair, but the pain lasted for only a few seconds before the fingers disappeared.

I could feel my hand slipping on the cloth as Reich pushed with all his strength so I let go quick and wrapped my arms around his whole body, giving him the kind of hug that we dreaded from my uncle Pietro whenever he had too much grappa in him. Reich tried to bounce his body off the floor and flailed his legs around, but he wasn't able to scissors me in any of those judo maneuvers that look so good in demonstrations, and I kept squeezing as hard as I could, my face not two inches from his, our eyes staring into each other like fighters do when the referee is giving them instructions.

I could feel the strength starting to leave my arms, and I knew that unless I got him within the next few seconds I was done. So I let go quickly and jammed the palm of my right hand under his chin as hard as I could, and his head snapped against the wall, the sound the same as when my father thumped a cantaloupe in his garden to see if it was ripe enough to cut. His eyes rolled up in the sockets so that all I could see was the milky white and when I let go of him his head slumped to the side. He was still breathing because I could hear the air being sucked in through his nose, but for the time being he was out of it.

THE BROKEN-HEARTED DETECTIVE

I was still lying on his body so I rolled off and pushed myself up on my knees to check on the other side of the room. Betty was sitting on the floor holding Bridget's head in her arms, her blouse drenched with blood. It looked the same as when a small girl rocks her dolly to sleep, in a world by herself, who knows what thoughts going through her mind. Bridget had died because of television. She had jumped through the door and yelled "Freeze" just like she had seen it on all the action shows. But she could no more have shot Reich than she could have jumped to the moon. It just wasn't in her to shoot somebody in either cold or hot blood. Her life had been spent saving people, not killing them. The Reichs of the world can cut you down in the blink of an eye, and forget about it even as they are doing it. She had intended to free us, which was what happened, but she had to pay the full fare for our trip.

Spread out on the floor right near me was Reich's underboss, Twining, and I could tell by the way his neck was twisted that he was dead. Standing by the door with two bodies in front of him was Brady, blood dripping from his wrists. "Jesus," I prayed aloud, as I realized what had happened. Brady had busted free from the nylon handcuffs. They had told us that no human being was strong enough to do this, but that had to have been what Brady had done. He was the one who had hauled Twining off me, and then he had taken care of the two that had come busting through the door. He was looking at Betty and Bridget, his face twisted into something between rage and sorrow. He had really liked that little lady, and when Reich tagged her, Brady went berserk enough to pull those handcuffs apart. It was something that couldn't be done. Never again would I believe that there was anything that couldn't be done.

I moved over to Betty and put my arms around her, the hot, heavy stink of the blood giving me a strange feeling in the pit of my stomach. When I looked into Betty's eyes, I realized that she was out of it, somewhere else, and I put my hand under her chin and pulled her face around to where she was looking right at me.

"Betty," I said, "you've got to let go of her. You've got to put her down."

"It's all because of me," she answered, "all of it. You, your family, Brady, and now Bridget. She's dead because she was my friend. I should be the one dead. It's my fault. All of it."

"It's not your fault," I told her. "It's his," and I pointed to where Reich was crumpled against the wall. Daphne wasn't stirring either, but I could see her chest moving up and down in regular movements, and I knew that she was going to be all right.

"How many more of them are out there?" Brady asked.

It took me a moment to clear my head.

"There were seven," I said. "Three are here. There have to be four more out there."

"Daphne got two outside," he said. "I saw them laying out there before they brought me in here. That leaves two in the house. What do you want to do now?"

"My mother," I said. "My mother's in the cellar. I'm going down to get her. You'll have to hold the fort until we get back."

"Take the AK47," he told me, "and keep your ass covered. They could be anywhere."

I picked up the gun, and then looked down at Betty who was still holding Bridget.

"I'll take care of it," said Brady. "Go get your ma."

There was no one in the corridor, and maybe I wasn't as careful as I should have been, but all I could think of was my mother down there in the dark in that box. There was nobody in the cellar so I moved quickly to where I had left her, pulled the cover apart and looked in. All I could see was that tiny, dark shape lying on the floor of the box.

"Ma," I said, the panic gripping my chest so bad that it hurt like angina. "Ma?"

She still didn't move, and I dropped the gun and fell to my knees beside her. She was breathing. I could hear it going in and out when I stuck my ear close to her nose.

"Ma," I said again, giving her a little shake. There was a slight shudder through her body, and then she said, "Vinnie?"

She'd been asleep. The poor lady had been so exhausted that she fell asleep.

"It's me, Ma," I told her. "I'm going to take you back upstairs now."

I backed out of the box and pulled her with me, then helped her stand up. When I let go, she didn't fall. I took her by the elbow and led her around the box, but there was a big coil of rope in the way, and I had to reverse our position before we had a clear path. Just as we reached the steps, I stopped.

"Wait here a second, Ma," I said, went back and picked up the rope.

The hall was still empty when we reached the top of the stairs, and Brady was peeking at me from around the corner of the doorway. When we got inside, I saw that they had found a blanket somewhere to cover Bridget, but there was still blood all over the floor and on Betty's blouse. Brady had pulled the two guys away from the doorway. One of them wasn't breathing, and the other one was snorting a peculiar sound so I knew he wouldn't be any trouble. Daphne was sitting up against the wall, and you could tell she was getting her strength back. Reich was where I had left him, but his eyelids were fluttering every few seconds.

"I brought this for him," I told Brady, and in a few minutes I had Reich wrapped like an Egyptian mummy. I hoped he would start itching someplace.

My mother had moved over to stand beside Betty, her right hand reaching out every once in a while as though she were going to touch her, but she never quite made it. Betty's face was that gray-white people get when they go into shock, and I wondered if I should get her down on the floor with her legs raised and a blanket over her. Brady was just standing there, staring down at the blanket covering Bridget. The blood on his wrists had dried, but he still looked like one of the attempted suicides we had to deal with all the time when we were on the force.

"Help!" Reich yelled, and I jumped around like someone had touched me with a cattle prod. Brady was as surprised as I was, but he immediately walked over, pinched Reich's nose shut and stuck his other hand over the mouth.

"Don't suffocate him," said Daphne from over by the wall. "He belongs to me."

Brady and I turned at the same moment to look at her. That was the deal we had made—we got Betty and she got Reich. I checked her face and saw that there was no mercy there, that he wasn't going to sweet talk her out of whatever she had planned. Brady and I looked at each other, and we didn't even have to nod. A deal was a deal.

"We've got to get some help." I said, "so somebody is going to have to trek out until they hit civilization."

"First we've got to see that the hacienda is clear," said Brady. "I'll go do that now."

"We'll both do it," I told him. "That way we'll cover it quicker."

Picking up Twining's gun from the floor, I handed it to Daphne who had pushed herself to her feet but was still leaning against the wall for support.

"Handle things until we get back," I said, "and make sure it's us coming down the hall."

She nodded, not quite ready to say something, but strength coming into her every second. If Reich had been wearing shoes, she would probably be dead, but luckily his bare feet hadn't done the damage they might.

"Okay," I said to Brady, "let's go."

But as we turned toward the door, Terry, Reich's nephew, came from around the corner and swept the room with an AK47 just like the one I was carrying. You could see that his finger was tight against the trigger.

"Nobody's going anywhere," he said.

38

"Terry," screamed Reich from behind me, "kill them! Kill them all."

My eyes were focused on the trigger finger, and I tensed myself for the jump when it started spitting bullets. But it didn't. The trigger pressure remained the same.

"Shoot, Terry," Reich ordered. "Do what I tell you."

I looked into Terry's eyes just as I had before in the hallway when he almost took off my ear. The same look was there, and I read it the same way. This boy was not a killer. But I had guessed wrong in the hall, and I could be just as wrong this time around.

"Put your guns on the floor," Terry commanded, the AK47 swinging in an arc big enough to cover us all. Daphne was to the side of him, and I think she would have gone for it if she was at full strength, but her hands were still shaking, and she finally dropped her gun to the floor the same as me and Brady.

"Cut me out of here, boy," ordered Reich, "but first make them all move against the other wall."

He knew damn well that Terry hadn't obeyed his first order, to kill us all, but he was going past it as if he had never said it. If the boy wouldn't kill, at least he would cut his uncle loose from the ropes. But Terry still didn't move, and Reich was getting nervous as well as impatient.

"Did you hear me, Terry?" he yelled. "After all I've done for you and your mother, you have no choice but to do what I say. You're my only heir, Terry. Everything I have will some day go to you. You can do anything you want; go anywhere you want; live any way you want. But first you have to cut me loose."

"If I do what you say, you'll kill them all, won't you?" Terry asked, and I let out my breath for the first time. He was talking instead of shooting, and he wasn't rushing over to free Uncle Kurt. I prayed for no sudden moves. If Brady or Daphne tried to jump him, he might start shooting from reflex action alone.

THE BROKEN-HEARTED DETECTIVE

"Terry," I said, "there's still a chance for you. You haven't killed anybody yet, and the government men aren't looking for you. If you make the wrong decision here, you could spend the rest of your life in jail."

"Don't listen to him," Reich shouted. "You and I are of the same blood. Your mother is my sister, and I have always provided for her since your father ran out on the two of you. I will give you a million dollars of your own. Five million. But first you have to turn me loose so we can get out of here. All I want to do is get out of here."

"You won't kill anybody?" Terry asked. "We'll just leave here?"

"That's all. We'll just get out of here. Nobody will be killed or even hurt. All we'll do is get out of here. But first you must get me loose."

"Terry," I said, "you know he's lying. If he gets a gun in his hand, he might even kill you along with the rest of us. You know he has no feelings for people. If he kills us, it will be on your head for the rest of your life, even if you escape. But the police will track you down eventually because there has been too much killing here already. If you let us go, we will tell the police that you had nothing to do with all this, that you were innocent of everything your uncle has done. They're out to get him, Terry, one way or another, and it would be best if you were clear of the whole mess. Now put down the gun, and let's have an end to all this killing."

"Don't listen to him," Reich screamed, spit running out of the sides of his mouth. He was straining against the ropes as though he could break through them the way Brady had with the handcuffs, but he was no Brady. In every way he was no Brady.

Terry started walking toward me, and I kept my eye on his finger as he moved, knowing that if he took two more steps, Brady would be able to jump him even as my body was falling to the floor. But he stopped short of where we needed him to be, and he looked right into my eyes the way he had in the hall.

"Here," he said, grabbing the muzzle of the gun with his left hand and turning it around so that the stock was facing me. "I don't want to kill anybody, and I don't want anybody to be killed."

I took the stock carefully in my left hand and pulled it away from him.

"No," Reich was screaming. "No! No! No!"

"Yes," I said in as steady a voice as I could manage. "Yes! Yes! Yes!"

Brady swung his fist into the side of the kid's head, and he went down like a stone. Betty gave a gasp, and I started to say something, but then I realized that we had to cover all the bases from then on, take no chances, clean it up and get out of there. No more Mr. Nice Guys.

"That makes six," said Brady. "Where do you think the other one is?"

"I don't know," I told him, "but we can't afford to have him getting the drop on us the way Terry did. As soon as Daphne's strong enough to hold down the fort, let's go flush him out."

"I'm all right now," said Daphne, moving away from the wall. She walked over to Reich and grabbed him by the hair on his head.

"Welcome back to mama, Kurt," she said, and banged his skull off the wall, just hard enough to hurt like hell but not enough to knock him out.

THE BROKEN-HEARTED DETECTIVE

"Listen," said Reich, "I can pay you millions if you let me go."

"Where are the tapes the government wants?" I asked him.

He thought about that for a few seconds.

"If I give them to you, will you let me go?" he asked.

"Let me put it this way," said Brady. "If you don't give them to us, you're going to wish you had given them to us."

"Wait a minute," said Daphne. "I'll be right back."

As she headed out the door, I said, "There's one more out there, Daphne. Be careful."

While she was gone, I went over to my mother, who was still hovering around Betty, who was staring down at the bloody blanket covering Bridget.

"You all right, Ma?" I asked her. She nodded and then moved her head to indicate Betty. I put my arm around Betty and squeezed just hard enough to get her attention.

"There's nothing you can do or say when something like this happens," I told her. "You just try and get through it as best you can."

She turned her face toward me.

"I can't cry," she said. "All that's in me is hate toward him because he caused all this, and hate toward me for getting everybody else involved. She'd be alive now if I hadn't mixed into her life. And none of you would have had to go through this horror. How can I ever make it up to any of you? What am I going to do?"

Before I could think up an answer that went beyond soothing sounds, Daphne returned, holding a large kitchen knife in her hands.

"Give me five minutes with him," she said, moving over to stand above Reich, "and I'll find out where the tapes and the money are, and anything else you want to know."

Reich knew her better than any of us.

"The tape, there's only the one, is hidden under my mattress," he said so quickly that his words tumbled over each other, "and the money is in the cellar behind a fake wall."

Brady couldn't help himself.

"Under the fucking mattress?" he said incredulously. "The superspy hides his goodies under the mattress?"

"Let's check the house and see if we can flush out the last guy," I said, "and then we have to see about getting us some help in here."

With Daphne guarding the room, Brady and I combed the place in classic police fashion, just as we had learned at training school. I even checked the box where I had hidden my mother. There was nobody to be found.

"He might have skipped," said Brady, "once he saw how things were going."

"We can't let up though," I said. "We've come this far and we can't let anything screw it up. We'll operate on the basis that the guy is still loose in the area."

Things were the same in the room when we returned, and it was time to consider the next step. The guy who had been breathing funny had quieted down, and Terry was starting to twitch himself awake.

"We've got to get help in here," I said to Brady. "Maybe we can get that jeep going and drive until we find a phone."

"The jeep is mine," said Daphne. "I have the keys and the valve spring, and that is how I am taking Kurt out of here."

THE BROKEN-HEARTED DETECTIVE

She also had a gun in her hand, a potent argument. Reasoning was needed.

"Daphne," I said, "we're not arguing about you and Kurt. But it's time to put an end to this whole business. We need medical help and transportation to get home. The jeep is all we have since you blew up the other three. How else are we going to establish contact with the outside?"

"The telephone," said my mother.

"What?"

"The telephone. He has one of those telephones like Dominic has when he wants to call somebody when he's out on a job."

A cellular phone. My brother Dominic, the contractor, was so proud of that phone that he took it to church sometimes. A cellular phone.

"Ma," I told her, "you're quite a smart lady."

And I kissed her right on top of the head.

39

It took a while to get through. There were no phone books in the house, and I had to dial information to get the number for the FBI.

When I asked the FBI operator to connect me with Agent Robert Yert, she put me on hold. A full minute later a man came on, and asked what I wanted.

"Agent Robert Yert," I told him.

"And what is this about?"

"Listen," I said, "and listen carefully. Are you taking notes?"

"You listen, whoever you are," he answered. "What is your business with Agent Yert?"

"Okay," I said, "I'm going to speak slowly so even you will understand. This is Vincent Altobelli. You tell Yert I have the goods he has been looking for. I'll hold on."

The guy was smarter than I was about to give him credit for.

"Hold on," he echoed to me, and then there was just the crackling noise from the goddamned cellular phone. The mountains must have made it tough to transmit the signals. It was a helluva convenience to have in a jam, however. I'd have to try my brother Dominic's one day. Maybe order a pizza while I was jogging in the park.

"Yert here," the telephone told me.

"We need help," I told him. "We've got Reich and the thing you were looking for, but we also have some wounded and some dead."

"This is an open line, for Christ's sake," Yert exploded.

"I don't give a goddamn if we're hooked into CNN," I told him. "We've got a desperate situation here, and you've got to get to us as quick as you can."

"Where are you?"

"We don't know."

"What do you mean you don't know?"

So then I told him about the tunnel and how far we had traveled, and what the canyon looked like.

"There are three burned-out jeeps in the courtyard," I told him.

"What the hell are you talking about?"

"There's been a war here, Yert, and we've got damages in people and property. We'll need ambulances as well as transportation, and there are prisoners as well as bodies."

"Will you for Christ's sake shut up?" he yelled. "How many are you?"

"Alive?"

There was a silence.

"Yes," he finally said.

"Seven or eight," I told him, "including my mother. Get word to my brother Petey that our mother's all right."

"I've got to round up a helicopter to scout the area until we locate you," he said. "Then some can be evacuated by helicopter, and we'll take the rest out by vehicles. But it may take a while to obtain the aircraft. Can you hold out all right?"

"We'll be all right until you get here," I said, "but the quicker the better."

"What number are you calling from?" he asked.

I looked at the phone and read him the number that was inserted into the little slot.

"I'll call you back as soon as we get squared away," he said. "Stay by the phone. Yert out."

I explained the situation to Brady and Daphne who were standing beside me. My mother finally had her arm around Betty, and they were sitting in the sun on the low wall around the terrace.

"I better get moving," said Daphne. "I want a good start before they get here."

"What are you talking about?" asked Brady. "Where are you going?"

She looked at him in surprise.

"I'm taking Kurt out of here," she said. "That was the deal."

"But the authorities will want him," said Brady. "He's going to do some hard time."

She turned so that she was directly facing me.

"Were you lying when we made our agreement?" she asked.

"I would have done anything to get Betty back safe and sound," I admitted.

"You have her back safe and sound," she said. "I've kept my part of the bargain. Now it's up to you to keep yours, or we settle it here one way or another."

She was still holding one of the Uzis in her hands, and I realized that she would go against us until somebody was dead if she didn't get what she wanted.

I looked at Brady, and he looked back at me.

"A deal's a deal," he said. "We always kept our word when we were working the streets."

"All right," I told her. "What do you want?"

"I need help in getting him into the jeep," she said, "and I'll want extra cans of gas. I want to get out of here as quick as I can before the government people arrive, and I need your word that you won't tell them in which direction I've gone."

"They'll track you down, Daphne," I said. "They're not going to let Reich get away after all he's put them through."

"He's not going to get away," she said. "He's going to be with me."

So we carried Reich out to the jeep, and then I rounded up some cans of gasoline, and Brady filled some water bottles. Daphne came out of the cellar carrying two suitcases, went back and came out with one more, which she could barely carry. She wedged the two lighter cases in the front and checked everything in the back where Reich was twisted around the gas cans.

"Don't let her take me away," he said, and it was as close to begging as a voice could get. "Keep me here for the government men. You'll be held responsible if they find me missing."

Just then Daphne came back carrying a shovel, which she threw in back with Reich.

"Don't let her take me," he said again, and she pinched his nose and then stuck a piece of cloth in when he was forced to open his mouth. "I'll take it out again when we get to where nobody is listening," she said, and somehow it gave me a shiver to hear her say it that way.

Just before she got in the driver's seat, she pulled the kitchen knife out of her belt and slipped it in beside the suitcases.

"That suitcase is for you two," she said, motioning to the one on the ground that she had barely been able to carry.

"What's in it?" asked Brady.

"Krugerrands," she said.

"What?"

"South African gold coins," she said. "They'd be too heavy for me to manage. These will do." And she patted the two suitcases in the front of the jeep.

"What will we do with them?" I asked her.

She shrugged.

"Whatever you want," she said. "That's up to you. You said you were private detectives. That's your fee."

She lifted the hood of the jeep and screwed in the

part she had removed. Then she pulled the key from inside her brassiere and started to get into the vehicle, but then stopped and turned toward us.

"You're good men," she said, "and I would be willing to work with you again. I know where you're from, and you may hear from me some time in the future. And then again you may not."

She started the motor and drove off to the east without looking back at us, and then turned left out of the canyon, and I hoped out of our lives forever.

"Do you think that was a threat or a promise?" I asked Brady.

"I don't know which way I want it to be," he said, and moved over to the suitcase on the sand. He lifted it up but I could see the strain in his shoulder.

"Jesus Christ," he said, "if these are what she said they are, we're millionaires."

"That's not our money," I told him.

"Yeah," he said. "Yeah."

I'll have to admit that it gave me a small satisfaction in my belly to hear the indecision in his voice because then he would know how I had felt about taking the money from Tony Pardo. He put it down and lifted it up and put it down again.

I turned and walked over to my mother and Betty to sit with them until the helicopter found us.

40

Despite keeping our eyes perpetually raised to the sky and our ears cocked, we saw and heard nothing for the next three hours. My mother went to the kitchen and put together a pretty good meal out of the canned stuff that was in the cupboards. It turned out she had been cooking for Reich's bunch the past two days. Reich had made her nervous, but she said the other guys treated her all right.

We fed Terry, who was handcuffed to a pipe in the cellar. The guy Brady had worked over when he rushed into the room while Reich and I were trying to kill each other was breathing, but he was still unconscious. Betty wouldn't eat no matter how much I coaxed her. I made her change her blouse for one of the men's shirts we found in a bureau, but she had insisted on going back to the room where Bridget lay, and was sitting on the floor beside her. The only way to have gotten her out of there was to drag her out, and neither Brady nor I were up to that.

I finally got the idea of piling all kinds of furniture in front of the terrace and making a fire that had a lot of smoke in it. About an hour after we lit that we heard the helicopter noise, and there it came over the mountain, a four-seater with Arizona National Guard markings on it.

Both Yert and Frye hopped out of it and ran toward us crouched low until they were well away from the whirring blades.

"Where are the tapes?" was the first thing they asked.

"We're all just fine," I told them.

They looked at me.

"We've got three dead people here," I said, "and one badly hurt. We've got my mother and Betty Wade just this side of exhaustion, and we've got a prisoner handcuffed in the basement. Where are the ambulances?"

"He's radioing our position now," said Frye, "and help will be here in a few hours. Where's Reich?"

Brady and I looked at each other.

"We don't know where he is right now," I said.

"What do you mean you don't know?" yelled Frye. "You said you had the tapes."

"We've got one tape," I told him, "and as far as we know that is all there is."

"That's what they thought in Washington," said Frye to Yert. "It's why things changed."

"How could you let him get away?" he asked, turning toward us again. "Why didn't you stop him?"

"It was out of our control," said Brady. "We had our hands full."

"Don't worry," said Frye to Yert. "He won't get far in this terrain. We'll have him one way or another by morning."

"I'm sure you will," I said. I shivered a little thinking how that one way or another might be. She had taken that butcher knife with her. But I wasn't sorry. Whatever Daphne did to him, and I mean whatever, he deserved. Too many times Brady and I had seen some piece of scum get away with what amounted to murder because society was bending over backward to protect his rights. I believed in our system despite its flaws, but for Reich I was willing to make an exception.

We showed the agents where the tape was hidden under the mattress, and they checked over the bodies and looked at the wounded guy in the coma and questioned Terry a little bit, and had all kinds of careful conversations over the cellular phone with various people in various places. It made me feel good to know that the charges were going on Reich's bill wherever his headquarters were. He wouldn't ever know about it, but it was enough that I knew about it.

We put in some good words for Terry, explaining that he could have wiped us out, and they said that everything would be taken into consideration, and we should note it down when our official statements were taken. I told them one of Reich's guys was unaccounted for, and they said they'd take care of that too.

Just before dark three cars and two ambulances showed up, and in one of the cars was my brother Petey. After he got through hugging and patting Ma, he started to give me a hard time about getting her into the mess in the first place. I just listened, saying nothing. When he ran out of words, he looked at me for a few seconds and then came over and gave me a big hug.

"You son of a bitch," he said, "are you all right?"

"Never felt better," I lied, and we grinned at each other and hugged again.

"The boys are all out of the hospital," he said, "and Pop will get out in two days. There's going to be a big party next week."

"And I'll bet Ma does the cooking," I said.

"Who else?"

Bridget and the dead guys were put in one ambulance, and my mother and the unconscious man in the other.

"Ma," I said, "it's all over. You'll never have to worry again."

She patted my hand.

"Vincent," she said, "it's time you found a nice Catholic girl and settled down."

Petey rode with her, and they took off just as dark was about to settle. The ambulance driver said it would be about four hours to get to Tucson after they reached the highway.

As I turned from watching the ambulance disappear, I saw Brady coming toward me lugging the suitcase Daphne had given him.

"They're leaving a couple of guys here for now," he said, "but they're ready for us to take off."

He put down the suitcase and then lifted it again to make sure I saw it, but I didn't say anything.

"Do you think we should take this with us?" he asked.

"It's up to you," I told him.

"Seriously," he said, "what do you think we should do?"

"It's all yours," I said. "I don't want any part of it."

"No, it's for both of us. Daphne said so."

"You do what you want," I told him. "Where's Betty?"

"In the house, I think."

I watched him lift the suitcase into the back of the sedan and follow it in. He had made his choice. I wondered what he would say if any of the agents asked him what was in the case.

I went back to the room where we'd had the showdown, but it was empty. I asked a couple of the agents

THE BROKEN-HEARTED DETECTIVE

if they had seen Betty, but none of them had noticed her. Yert and Frye were looking at the video tape in Reich's bedroom, and they switched off the set when I came in and told me to get the hell out of there. I asked them if they had seen Betty, but they also said no. They told me they would take care of all the arrangements for the dead people and warned me not to say anything about what had really happened.

"What about Bridget?" I asked.

"Who?"

"The nurse who was murdered by Reich."

"We'll take care of that too."

All I could do was look at them. Bridget was about to be killed in an automobile accident or something like that. A classic spook cover-up. What could you say to people like that?

I went through every room in the house, but Betty was nowhere to be found, and I began to panic as it got darker and darker. I ran out of the house yelling, "Betty, Betty," but there was no answer. I don't know why, but I took off for the strip of brush where we had hidden before we had gone to the house, and when I came around the corner, there she was, picking up things from the ground and wrapping them in a blanket. When I got closer, I could see that it was stuff that had belonged to Bridget.

The dark came down like it does in the desert, and it took my eyes a few seconds to adjust to the dim light from the moon.

"It's time to go," I told her, taking the rolled blanket from her hands.

"Go where?" she asked.

"Back to Tucson. Back to our lives."

I could see she was crying, so I reached out my right arm to pull her close.

"It's over now," I told her. "We can go back to San Bernardino."

"I can't stay in Tucson," she said. "It's going to be bad wherever I go, but I can't stay there."

"We're never going to forget any of this," I said, "but we're alive and we'll go on living. And as the good new things happen, all this will become a little dimmer. It won't disappear, it will never disappear, but we'll get married and there will be happy things that will take up some of the room."

I felt her draw back.

"You want to marry me, Altobelli?"

I looked at her, not knowing what to say at first. What do you say to someone who hasn't recognized the obvious.

"Sure. Sure I want to marry you. Don't you want to marry me?"

"If that's what you want."

A little shiver went through me and that cold feeling grabbed hold of my belly.

"Isn't it what you want?" I asked, holding my breath after I stopped. The silence went on so long that I had to let it out again.

"Yes," she finally said, "I'd like to be married to you."

"I love you," I told her.

"And I love you."

"We'll have a big church wedding," I said, "and my brothers—"

"Wait a minute," she stopped me. "No church wedding. I told you I don't believe in organized religion. We'll have a civil ceremony and then—"

"My mother would die if we didn't have a Catholic wedding," I said.

"Are you saying that I would have to become a Catholic?"

"Not necessarily a Catholic, but there are certain things . . ."

"Altobelli, I would never become a Catholic, and I would never get married in a church. Never."

"But . . ."

"Listen to me, Altobelli," she said. "I owe you my life. I love you. I don't know how much of it is what they call love love, and how much is gratitude love, but I would be happy to spend the rest of my life with you and have kids and all the rest. But I will not become Catholic, or bring my kids up Catholic, or get married in a church in the first place. If you want, we can live together for a while to see how it works out. Then we can talk about marriage."

"But my mother—"

"Your mother would be upset if we were living together. Is that what you're saying? It's got to be church or nothing?"

"Well, she—"

"We don't have to stay in San Bernardino, Altobelli. I'll go anywhere with you, and love you and take care of you, married or unmarried. But as much as I owe you and love you, I cannot change something that is such a part of my life and being. I just can't do it."

"Are you an atheist?" I asked her, wanting to kick myself as the words came out of my mouth.

"I don't know what the hell I am," she answered, "but that's how I am."

"Betty," I said, "you're giving me no choices. You're saying it's you or my mother, that I can't have both. I can't hurt her anymore. She's been through enough."

"I am giving you choices," she said. "I've given you all kinds of choices. There's even the choice of never seeing me again. I hope you pick the choice that includes me in your life, but if it's me you love, then you must take me as I am. I can't fake any religious bullshit. I can't fake anything. It's your choice."

From the house I could hear Yert yelling for me, saying it was time to go, but I was stuck on the spot in the dark in the desert.

I went over all the choices in my mind. Betty. No Betty. My mother. My mother if I didn't get married in a church. If I didn't marry a Catholic. My mother if I lived in sin without getting married. My family. Could I live without my family? Could I live without Betty?

Choices.

I looked down at her face in the dim light. She was so exhausted she could barely breathe, and she had probably never looked worse. But she was also never more beautiful.

Yert or Frye had found Reich's electric bullhorn and was yelling into the darkness.

"Altobelli, are you coming or not? Make up your mind, Altobelli. Make up your mind."

Make up my mind. Make up my mind.

"They're waiting for us," I said, taking her arm and leading the way to the car, which had its motor running and lights on.

Yert was driving, with Frye sitting beside him. I opened the right rear door, helped Betty into the seat, closed the door and went around to the other side. We started off without anybody saying anything, but then Yert and Frye started talking to each other in spook language that we weren't supposed to understand. It had to do with the kind of report they were going to file, and how they had to get together on the story that was going to be told to their bosses. Not having Reich was obviously their biggest problem when it came to their future with the agencies.

In the dark all I could see was Betty's profile as she sat there like a statue with nothing to show that she was even breathing. She didn't know if it was love love or gratitude love. She had saved my life and now I had been part of saving hers, so basically we were even, shake hands and walk away. Could I give up my family for a woman who wasn't even sure how she loved me? Would I spend the rest of my life wondering, trying to decipher each word, each action? It had taken me a while to get over Carlotta. Would I be able to get over Betty?

But then I thought of my mother and what she had gone through because of me, and my brothers and how they could have died in the accident, and I knew I couldn't abandon my family no matter how much I loved this woman. *Basta!* as my uncle Pietro would say when the final decision had been made on anything, even if it was just about what kind of pasta to throw in the boiling water. I could feel my stomach knot itself into a ball as I thought about never seeing Betty Wade again. But if she was going to be like a stone, I had to be like a rock.

"Altobelli," she said, making my heart jump with surprise.

"Yes?"

"If I come back to San Bernardino, would you put

me up until I found my own place to live? It wouldn't be for long. I just don't want to be alone for a while."

My heart gave another jump. Which should I be? Happy? Or sad? Would it lead to a solution, or just make it double tough for everybody? I remembered something Carlotta had said to me in bed one time when I told her I didn't think I was up to another go-round. *You can have your cake and eat it too,* she had said. *You just have to eat it very, very slowly.* Maybe if I just went slowly, slowly, for a while some miracle might take place.

"No problem," I said, taking her hand and squeezing it hard enough to let her know how I felt about her, but softly enough so she could realize I wasn't shoving. "No problem at all."

Christ, I said to myself, *have you got problems!*

JEROME DOOLITTLE

TOM BETHANY MYSTERIES

BODY SCISSORS

STRANGE HOLD

BEAR HUG

HEAD LOCK

and don't miss

HALF NELSON

Available in Hardcover from

POCKET BOOKS

582-02

"Jeremiah Healy writes the private-eye novel as it should be written, taut and tough, with a convincingly professional hero and a story that hits the ground running and accelerates from there."
—*San Diego Union-Tribune*

Jeremiah Healy

FOURSOME
BLUNT DARTS
RIGHT TO DIE
SHALLOW GRAVES
SO LIKE SLEEP
STAKED GOAT
SWAN DIVE
YESTERDAY'S NEWS

POCKET BOOKS

**Available
from Pocket Books**

829-01